PUFFIN BOOKS

THE PUFFIN BOOK OF SCIENCE FICTION

Nicholas Fisk has been an actor, jazz musician, illustrator, photographer, copywriter, publisher and, from the age of nine, a writer. He believes that almost any imaginable possibility may become a reality within the lifetime of someone who is young now. This century has already seen more changes and discoveries than any other – and the rate of change gets faster every day.

The Puffin Book of
Science Fiction

STORIES CHOSEN BY

NICHOLAS FISK

Illustrated by Nick Harris

PUFFIN BOOKS

PUFFIN BOOKS

Published by the Penguin Group
Penguin Books Ltd, 27 Wrights Lane, London W8 5TZ, England
Penguin Books USA Inc., 375 Hudson Street, New York, New York 10014, USA
Penguin Books Australia Ltd, Ringwood, Victoria, Australia
Penguin Books Canada Ltd, 10 Alcorn Avenue, Toronto, Ontario, Canada M4V 3B2
Penguin Books (NZ) Ltd, 182–190 Wairau Road, Auckland 10, New Zealand

Penguin Books Ltd, Registered Offices: Harmondsworth, Middlesex, England

First published by Viking 1993
Published in Puffin Books 1994
3 5 7 9 10 8 6 4 2

Printed in England by Clays Ltd, St Ives plc
Filmset in Bembo

Contents

Introduction

S *cience Fiction.* What a miserable description! *Science*, a stone-cold word; added to *fiction*, another chiller. No wonder so many people turned away from SF stories.

- But then came the block-buster science fiction films: *Star Wars, Close Encounters* and all the others. Suddenly you *had* to like SF, even if you didn't; and it was much the same a century ago when Jules Verne and (particularly) H G Wells lit the flame. It flickered on among enthusiasts (though there were not all that many of them) for several decades; became a minor cult in the 1930s, '40s and '50s; then – WHOOOMPF! – there came the great cinematic flare-up of our time. Hooray for the film-makers.

Yet even today science fiction is hard to define. Just what *is* it? Spaceships, alien beings, monsters? Yes, if you like. But SF writers seem to cover every conceivable or inconceivable human or non-human field of imagination: the innermost workings of human minds, bodies and souls ... new folklores ... history re-written ... even *The Nine Billion Names of God*. The following poem, possibly the shortest in our language, nevertheless poses a question of interest to every SF fan ...

I

Why?

So what is the proper definition of science fiction? I slide out of answering the question in this way. It isn't SF at all. It is IF – plain old if ...

IF there were a robot servant in your home ... IF we were still ruled by our Roman invaders ... IF we could talk to animals, and they to us ... IF we could buy tickets to travel in time ... IF the internal-combustion engine had never been invented ...

IF, IF, IF!

IF the world is to end next Tuesday ... IF we are visited by alien beings ... IF we are about to swap high-tech for mystical powers, and turn the lights on or off simply by wishing ...

IF is the starting point. Proceed from there.

This book samples the works of writers who have done just that. In selecting the entries, no rules were followed; no divisions of Ancient and Modern; no worries about the constantly changing state of the art. For though the term 'science fiction' belongs to this century, the minds and skills that go into the SF brew stretch back to cavemen's drawings. We *think* those drawings were a form of magic: 'IF I draw this beast well, when I come to hunt it, it will be mine'. If only we could talk to that caveman . . .

IF, IF, IF!

Nicholas Fisk

The Clipper of the Clouds   JULES VERNE

The Clipper of the Clouds

JULES VERNE

Jules Verne, a Frenchman, was perhaps the first giant of science fiction. Today he is universally saluted but seldom, if ever, read. His style, characters and content have not aged well. But his 'hardware', his mechanical inventions – great balloons, palatial submarines, the sumptuous Clipper of the Clouds – still fascinate us after 130 years or more.

From *The War of the Worlds*

H G WELLS

H G Wells was the father-figure and pioneer of science fiction. His major SF works include *The War of the Worlds*, *The First Men on the Moon* and *The Time Machine*. His 'trick', if you can call it that, was to set a fascinating and outrageous idea in a frame of common-place reality: extraordinary events, ordinary people.

The War of the Worlds was first published in 1898. No doubt someone, somewhere, is today preparing yet another film or TV version.

We remained at Weybridge until midday, and at that hour we found ourselves at the place near Shepperton Lock where the Wey and Thames join. Part of the time we spent helping two old women to pack a little cart. The Wey has a treble mouth, and at this point boats are to be hired, and there was a ferry across the river. On the Shepperton side was an inn, with a lawn, and beyond that the tower of Shepperton Church – it has been replaced by a spire – rose above the trees.

Here we found an excited and noisy crowd of fugitives. As yet the flight had not grown to a panic, but there were already far more people than all the boats going to and fro could enable to cross. People came panting along under heavy burdens; one husband and wife were even carrying a small outhouse door between them, with some of their household goods piled thereon. One man told us he meant to try to get away from Shepperton Station.

There was a lot of shouting, and one man was even jesting. The idea people seemed to have here was that the Martians were simply formidable human beings, who might attack and sack the town, to be certainly destroyed in the end. Every now and then people would glance nervously across the Wey, at the meadows towards Chertsey, but everything over there was still.

Across the Thames, except just where the boats landed, everything was quiet, in vivid contrast with the Surrey side. The people who landed there from the boats went tramping off down the lane. The big ferry-boat had just made a journey. Three or four soldiers stood on the lawn of the inn, staring and jesting at the fugitives, without offering to help.

The inn was closed, as it was now within prohibited hours.

'What's that!' cried a boatman, and 'Shut up, you fool!' said a man near me to a yelping dog. Then the sound came again, this time from the direction of Chertsey, a muffled thud – the sound of a gun.

The fighting was beginning. Almost immediately unseen batteries across the river to our right, unseen because of the trees, took up the chorus, firing heavily one after the other. A woman screamed. Everyone stood arrested by the sudden stir of battle, near us and yet invisible to us. Nothing was to be seen save flat meadows, cows feeding unconcernedly for the most part, and silvery pollard willows motionless in the warm sunlight.

'The sojers 'll stop 'em,' said a woman beside me doubtfully. A haziness rose over the tree-tops.

Then suddenly we saw a rush of smoke far away up the river, a puff of smoke that jerked up into the air, and hung, and forthwith the ground heaved underfoot and a heavy explosion shook the air, smashing two or three windows in the houses near, and leaving us astonished.

'Here they are!' shouted a man in a blue jersey. 'Yonder! D'yer see them? Yonder!'

Quickly, one after the other, one, two, three, four of the armoured Martians appeared, far away over the little trees, across the flat meadows that stretch towards Chertsey, and striding hurriedly towards the river. Little cowled figures they seemed at first, going with a rolling motion and as fast as flying birds.

Then, advancing obliquely towards us, came a fifth. Their armoured bodies glittered in the sun, as they swept swiftly forward upon the guns, growing rapidly larger as they drew nearer. One on the extreme left, the remotest, that is, flourished a huge case high in the air, and the ghostly terrible Heat-Ray I had already seen on Friday night smote towards Chertsey, and struck the town.

At sight of these strange, swift and terrible creatures, the crowd along by the water's edge seemed to me to be for a moment horror-struck. There was no screaming or shouting, but a silence. Then a hoarse murmur and a movement of feet – a splashing from the water. A man, too frightened to drop the portmanteau he carried on his shouder, swung round and sent me staggering with a blow from the corner of his burden. A woman thrust at me with her hand and rushed past me. I turned, too, with the rush of the people, but I was not too terrified for thought. The terrible Heat-Ray was in my mind. To get under water! That was it!

'Get under water!' I shouted unheeded.

I faced about again, and rushed towards the approaching Martian – rushed right down the gravelly beach and headlong into the water. Others did the same. A boatload of people putting back came leaping out as I rushed past. The stones under my feet were muddy and slippery, and the river was so low that I ran perhaps twenty feet scarcely waist-deep. Then, as the Martian towered overhead scarcely a couple of hundred yards away, I flung myself forward under the surface. The splashes of the people in the boats leaping into the river sounded like thunderclaps in my ears. People were landing hastily on both sides of the river.

But the Martian machine took no more notice for the moment of the people running this way and that than a man would of the confusion of ants in a nest against which his foot has kicked. When, half-suffocated, I raised my head above water the Martian's hood pointed at the batteries that were still firing across the river, and as it advanced it swung loose what must have been the generator of the Heat-Ray.

In another moment it was on the bank, and in a stride wading half-way across. The knees of its foremost legs bent at the further bank, and in another moment it had raised itself to its full height again, close to the village of Shepperton. Forthwith the six guns, which, unknown to anyone on the right bank, had been hidden behind the outskirts of that village, fired simultaneously. The sudden near concussions, the last close upon the first, made my heart jump. The monster was already raising the case generating the Heat-Ray as the first shell burst six yards above the hood.

I gave a cry of astonishment. I saw and thought nothing of the other four Martian monsters: my attention was riveted upon the nearer incident. Simultaneously two other shells burst in the air near the body as the hood twisted round in time to receive, but not in time to dodge, the fourth shell.

The shell burst clean in the face of the thing. The hood bulged, flashed, was whirled off in a dozen tattered fragments of red flesh and glittering metal.

'Hit!' shouted I, with something between a scream and a cheer.

I heard answering shouts from the people in the water about me. I could have leapt out of the water with that momentary exultation.

The decapitated colossus reeled like a drunken giant: but it did not fall over. It recovered its balance by a miracle, and, no longer heeding its steps, and with the camera that fired the Heat-Ray now rigidly upheld, it reeled swiftly upon Shepperton. The living intelligence, the Martian within the hood, was slain and splashed to the four winds of heaven, and the thing was now but a mere intricate device of metal whirling to destruction. It drove along in a straight line, incapable of guidance. It struck the tower of Shepperton Church, smashing it down as the impact of a battering-ram might have done, swerved aside, blundered on, and collapsed with a tremendous impact into the river out of my sight.

A violent explosion shook the air, and a spout of water, steam, mud, and shattered metal, shot far up into the sky. As the camera of the Heat-Ray hit the water, the latter had incontinently flashed into steam. In another moment a huge wave, like a muddy tidal bore, but almost scaldingly hot, came sweeping round the bend upstream. I saw people struggling shore-wards, and heard their screaming and shouting faintly above the seething and roar of the Martian's collapse.

For the moment I heeded nothing of the heat, forgot the patent need of self-preservation. I splashed through the tumultuous water, pushing aside a man in black to do so, unto until I could see round the bend. Half a dozen deserted boats pitched aimlessly upon the confusion of the waves. The fallen Martian came into sight downstream, lying across the river, and for the most part submerged.

Thick clouds of steam were pouring off the wreckage, and through the tumultuously whirling wisps I could see, intermittently and vaguely, the gigantic limbs churning the water and flinging a splash and spray of mud and froth into the air. The tentacles swayed and struck like living arms, and, save for the helpless purposelessness of these movements, it was as if some wounded thing struggled for life amidst the waves. Enormous quantities of a ruddy brown fluid were spurting up in noisy jets out of the machine.

My attention was diverted from this sight by a furious yelling, like that of the thing called a siren in our manufacturing towns. A man, knee-deep near the towing-path, shouted inaudibly to me and pointed. Looking back, I saw the other Martians advancing with gigantic strides down the riverbank from the direction of Chertsey. The Shepperton guns spoke this time unavailingly.

At that I ducked at once under water, and, holding my breath until movement was an agony, blundered painfully along under the surface as long as I could. The water was in a tumult about me, and rapidly growing hotter.

When for a moment I raised my head to take breath, and throw the hair and water from my eyes, the steam was rising in a whirling white fog that at first hid the Martians altogether. The noise was deafening. Then I saw them dimly, colossal figures of grey, magnified by the mist. They had passed by me, and two were stooping over the frothing tumultuous ruins of their comrade.

The third and fourth stood beside him in the water, one perhaps 200 yards from me, the other towards Laleham. The generators of the Heat-Rays waved high, and the hissing beams smote down this way and that.

The air was full of sound, a deafening and confusing conflict of noises, the clangorous din of the Martians, the crash of falling houses, the thud of trees, fences, sheds, flashing into flame, and the crackling and roaring of fire. Dense black smoke was leaping up to mingle with the steam from the river, and as the Heat-Ray went to and fro over Weybridge, its impact was marked by flashes of incandescent white, that gave place at once to a smoky dance of lurid flames. The nearer houses still stood intact, awaiting their fate, shadowy, faint, and pallid in the steam, with the fire behind them going to and fro.

For a moment, perhaps, I stood there, breast-high in the almost boiling water, dumbfounded at my position, hopeless of escape. Through the reek I could see the people who had been with me in the river scrambling out of the water through the reeds, like little frogs hurrying through grass from the advance of a man, or running to and fro in utter dismay on the towing-path.

Then suddenly the white flashes of the Heat-Ray came leaping towards me. The houses caved in as they dissolved at its touch, and darted out flames; the trees changed to fire with a roar. It flickered up and down the towing-path, licking off the people who ran this way and that, and came down to the water's edge not fifty yards from where I stood. It swept across the river to Shepperton, and the water in its track rose in a boiling wheal crested with steam. I turned shoreward.

In another moment the huge wave, well-nigh at the boiling-point, had rushed upon me. I screamed aloud, and scalded, half-blinded, agonized, I staggered through the leaping, hissing water towards the shore. Had my foot stumbled, it would have been the end. I fell helplessly, in full sight of the Martians, upon the broad, bare gravelly spit that runs down to mark the angle of the Wey and Thames. I expected nothing but death.

I have a dim memory of the foot of a Martian coming down within a score of yards of my head, driving straight into the loose gravel, whirring it this way and that, and lifting again; of a long suspense, and then of the four carrying the debris of their comrade between them, now clear, and then presently faint, through a veil of smoke, receding interminably, as it seemed to me, across a vast space of river and meadow. And then, very slowly, I realized that by a miracle I had escaped.

From *The Horror of the Heights*

ARTHUR CONAN DOYLE

Conan Doyle? Why, everyone knows he was the creator of Sherlock Holmes! What else?

In fact, there is a great deal of 'what else'. Dr Conan Doyle was endlessly productive. He wrote science fiction long before the term was invented. *The Horror of the Heights* was written just after World War One. It is interesting to note, in this age of jet engines with fantastic power, that the story's narrator uses a monoplane ('There's nothing like a monoplane ... it doesn't mind damp.') with an advanced engine – 'a ten cylinder rotary working up to one hundred and seventy-five (horsepower)'. Only twenty years later, fighter aircraft could call on ten times that power. While today's aeroplanes ...

The man telling this story is a gentleman-amateur of Victorian science and aviation. He is flying his monoplane . . .

'These air–snakes were of a very light grey or smoke colour, with some darker lines within, which gave the impression of a definite organism. One of them whisked past my very face, and I was conscious of a cold, clammy contact, but their composition was so unsubstantial that I could not connect them with any thought of physical danger, any more than the beautiful bell–like creatures which had preceded them. There was no more solidity in their frames than in the floating spume from a broken wave.

'But a more terrible experience was in store for me. Floating downwards from a great height there came a purplish patch of vapour, small as I saw it first, but rapidly enlarging as it approached me, until it appeared to be hundreds of square feet in size. Though fashioned of some transparent, jelly–like substance, it was none the less of much more definite outline and solid consistence than anything which I had seen before. There were more traces, too, of a physical organization, especially two vast shadowy, circular plates upon either side, which may have been eyes, and a perfectly solid white projection between them which was as curved and cruel as the beak of a vulture.

'The whole aspect of this monster was formidable and threatening, and it kept changing its colour from a very light mauve to a dark, angry purple so thick that it cast a shadow as it drifted between my monoplane and the sun. On the upper curve of its huge body there were three great projections which I can only describe as enormous bubbles, and I was convinced as I looked at them that they were charged with some extremely light gas which served to buoy up the misshapen and semi-solid mass in the rarefied air. The creature moved swiftly along, keeping pace easily with the monoplane, and for twenty miles or more it formed my horrible escort, hovering over me like a bird of prey which is waiting to pounce. Its method of progression – done so swiftly that it was not easy to follow – was to throw out a long, glutinous streamer in front of it, which in turn seemed to draw forward the rest of the writhing body. So elastic and gelatinous was it, that never for two successive minutes was it the same shape, and yet each change made it more threatening and loathsome than the last.

'I knew that it meant mischief. Every purple flush of its hideous body told me so. The, vague, goggling eyes which were turned always upon me were cold and merciless in their viscid hatred. I dipped the nose of my monoplane downwards to escape it. As I did so, as quick as a flash there shot out a long tentacle from this mass of floating blubber, and it fell as light and sinuous as a whiplash across the front of my machine. There was a loud hiss as it lay for a moment across the hot engine, and whisked itself into the air again, while the huge flat body drew itself together as if in sudden pain. I dipped to a vol-piqué, but again a tentacle fell over the monoplane and was shorn off by the propeller as easily as it might have cut through a smoke wreath. A long, gliding, sticky, serpent-like coil came from behind and caught me round the waist, dragging me out of the fuselage. I tore at it, my fingers sinking into the smooth, glue-like surface, and for an instant I disengaged myself, but only to be caught round the boot by another coil, which gave me a jerk that tilted me almost to my back.

'As I fell over I blazed off both barrels of my gun, though, indeed, it was like attacking an elephant with a pea-shooter to imagine that any human weapon could cripple that mighty bulk. And yet I aimed better than I knew, for, with a loud report, one of the great blisters upon the creature's back exploded with the puncture of the buckshot. It was very clear that my conjecture was right, and that these vast clear bladders were distended with some lifting gas, for in an instant the huge cloud-like body turned sideways, writhing desperately to find its balance, while the white beak snapped and gaped in horrible fury. But already I had shot away on the steepest glide that I dared to attempt, my engine still full on, the flying propeller and the force of gravity shooting me downwards like an aerolite. Far behind me I saw a dull, purplish smudge growing swiftly smaller and merging into the blue sky behind it. I was safe out of the deadly jungle of the outer air.

'Once out of danger I throttled my engine, for

nothing tears a machine to pieces quicker than running on full power from a height. It was a glorious spiral vol-plané from nearly eight miles of altitude– first, to the level of the silver cloud-bank, then to that of the storm-cloud beneath it, and finally, in beating rain, to the surface of the earth. I saw the Bristol Channel beneath me as I broke from the clouds, but, having still some petrol in my tank, I got twenty miles inland before I found myself stranded in a field half a mile from the village of Ashcombe. There I got three tins of petrol from a passing motor car, and at ten minutes past six that evening I alighted gently in my own home meadow at Devizes, after such a journey as no mortal upon earth has ever yet taken and lived to tell the tale. I have seen the beauty and I have seen the horror of the heights – and greater beauty or greater horror than that is not within the ken of man.'

From *The Space Merchants*

FREDERICK POHL and C M KORNBLUTH

Frederick Pohl and the late C M Kornbluth often worked as one man – apparently almost telepathically. This excerpt is taken from *The Space Merchants*, first published (with huge success) some forty years ago. The main plank of the plot is simple: rival advertising agencies in Madison Avenue, New York, dominate national and international affairs. How, you might ask, are things going today?

Our 'hero', once an advertising executive, has lost his way: now he must serve as assistant to the Master Slicer of Chicken Little, a huge lump of living protein – artificial mainstay of the city's diet . . .

The aristocrat of Dorm Ten was Herrera. After ten years with Chlorella he had worked his way up – topographically it was down – to Master Slicer. He worked in the great, cool vault underground, where Chicken Little grew and was cropped by him and other artisans. He swung a sort of two handed sword that carved off great slabs of the tissue, leaving it to the lesser packers and trimmers and their faceless helpers to weight it, shape it, freeze it, cook it, flavour it, package it, and ship it off to the area on quota for the day.

He had more than a production job. He was a safety valve. Chicken Little grew and grew, as she had been growing for decades. Since she had started as a lump of heart tissue, she didn't know any better than to grow up against a foreign body and surround it. She didn't know any better than to grow and fill her concrete vault and keep growing, compressing her cells and rupturing them. As long as she got nutrient, she grew. Herrera saw to it that she grew round and plump, that no tissue got old and tough before it was sliced, that one side was not neglected for the other.

With this responsibility went commensurate pay, and yet Herrera had not taken a wife or an apartment in one of the upper tiers of the pylon. He made trips that were the subject of bawdy debate while he was gone – and which were never referred to without careful politeness while he was present. He kept his two-handed slicer by him at all times, and often idly sleeked its edge with a hone. He was a man I had to know. He was a man with money – he *must* have money after ten years – and I needed it.

The pattern of the B labour contract had become quite clear. You never got out of debt. Easy credit was part of the system, and so were irritants that forced you to exercise it. If I fell behind ten dollars a week I would owe one thousand one hundred dollars to Chlorella at the end of my contract, and would have to work until the debt was wiped out. And while I worked, a new debt would accumulate.

I needed Herrera's money to buy my way out of Chlorella and back to New York: Kathy, my wife; Venus Section, my job.

Days went by like weeks. Herrera talked little to me, until one evening in the day-room he suddenly asked: 'You ever see *Gallina*?' That was Chicken Little. I said no. 'Come on down, then. I can get you in. She's a sight.'

We walked through corridors and leapt for the descending cargo net. I resolutely shut my eyes. You look straight down that thing and you get the high-shy horrors. Forty, Thirty, Twenty, Ten, Zero, Minus Ten –

'Jump off, Jorge,' Herrera said. 'Below Minus Ten is the machinery.' I jumped.

Minus Ten was gloomy and sweated water from its concrete walls. The roof was supported by immense beams. A tangle of pipes jammed the corridor where we got off. 'Nutrient fluid,' Herrera said.

I asked about the apparently immense weight of the ceiling. 'Concrete and lead. It shields cosmic rays. Sometimes a *Gallina* goes cancer.' He spat. 'No good to eat for people. You got to burn it all if you don't catch it real fast and –' He swung his glittering slicer in a screaming arc to show me what he meant by 'catch'.

He swung open a door. 'This is her nest,' he said proudly. I looked and gulped.

It was a great concrete dome, concrete-floored. Chicken Little filled most of it. She was a grey-brown, rubbery hemisphere some fifteen yards in diameter. Dozens of pipes ran into her pulsating flesh. You could see that she was alive.

Herrera said to me: 'All day I walk around her. I see a part growing fast, it looks good and tender, I slice.' His two-handed blade screamed again. This time it shaved off an inch thick Chicken Little steak. 'Crumbs behind me hook it away and cut it up and put it on the conveyor.' There were tunnel openings spotted around the circumference of the dome, with conveyor belts visible in them.

'Doesn't she grow at night?'

'No. They turn down the nutrient just enough, they let the waste accumulate in her just right. Each night she almost dies. Each morning she comes to life like San Lázaro. But nobody ever pray before *probrecita Gallina*, hey?' He whacked the rubbery thing affectionately with the flat of his slicer.

'You like her,' I said inanely.

'Sure, Jorge. She does tricks for me.' He looked around and then marched the circuit of the nest, peering into each of the tunnel mouths. Then he took a short beam from one of them and casually braced it against the door to the nest. It fitted against a crossbar on the door and against a seemingly-random groove in the concrete floor. It would do very well as a lock.

'I'll show you the trick,' he said, with an Aztec grin. With a magician's elaborate gesture he took from his pocket a sort of whistle. It didn't have a mouthpiece. It had an air tank fed by a small hand pump. 'I didn't make this,' he hastened to assure me. 'They call it Galton's whistle, but who this Galton is I don't know. Watch – and listen.'

He began working the pump, pointing the whistle purposefully at Chicken Little. I heard no sound, but I shuddered as the rubbery protoplasm bulged in away from the pipe in a hemispherical depression.

'Don't be scared, *compañero*,' he told me. 'Just follow.' He pumped harder and passed me a flashlight which I stupidly turned on. Herrera played the soundless blast of the whistle against Chicken Little like a hose. She reacted with a bigger cavity that finally became an archway whose floor was the concrete floor of the nest.

Herrera walked into the archway, saying: 'Follow.' I did, my heart pounding frightfully. He inched forward, pumping the whistle, and the archway became a dome. The entrance into Chicken Little behind us became smaller . . . smaller . . . smaller . . .

We were quite inside, in a hemispherical bubble moving slowly through a hundred-ton lump of grey-brown rubbery flesh. 'Light on the floor, *compañero*,' he said, and I flashed it on the floor. The concrete was marked with lines that looked accidental, but which guided Herrera's feet. We inched forward, and I wondered vividly what would happen if the Galton whistle sprang a leak . . .

After about two thousand years of inch-by-inch progress my light flashed in a crescent of metal. Herrera piped the bubble over it, and it became a disc. Still pumping, he stamped three times on it. It flipped open like a manhole. 'You first,' he said, and I dived into it, not knowing or caring whether the landing was hard or soft. It was soft, and I lay there, shuddering. A moment later Herrera landed beside me and the manhole above me clapped shut. He stood up, massaging his arm. 'Hard work,' he said. 'I pump and pump that thing and I don't hear it. Some day it's going to stop working and I won't know the difference until –'. He grinned again.

From *Captain Courage and the Rose Street Gang*

JAN MARK

Jan Mark is rightly regarded as a serious, a literary, a highly skilled, writer for children. She wins prizes for deeply considered works such as *The Ennead*.

So she cannot be wildly funny, can she? And she is not likely to get exactly right the feeling of our day and ways, is she? No, of course not . . .

Jan Mark lives and works in England.

Arty said, 'I want to play in the street.'

Arty's mother said, 'For heaven's sake stop whining and get out from under my feet.'

Arty squeezed past her, between the home laundry unit where the week's washing was twirling in its drum, and the fast food module, into the leisure area.

There was not very much more space in there, for his elder brother Lance was lying on the floor playing chess with PREM, his Programmed Response Module. PREM was an early model and had acquired a reciprocal twitch every time it extended its articulated limb to move a chess piece. Consequently it was continually backing away from the board, propelled in a leftward curve by the thrust of its single right arm. Lance, on his stomach, followed it round the room, pushing the chess board in front of him like a tray. He had been playing for only twenty minutes and he was already on his second circuit. PREM accelerated irritably. It was losing, and its programmed responses did not include good sportsmanship.

Arty said, 'Lance, why don't we go and play in the street?'

'Too far,' Lance said, shortly. 'Anyway, it may be raining.'

'I bet it's not.'

'It may be by the time we get there.'

Arty went to the Factcentre console and dialled Weatherdata; a map of South-East England appeared on the screen. Arty pressed the Locale key and the map dissolved into a close-up of Maidstone. He adjusted the volume control and a cheery voice chipped in: 'Good morning, Dataseeker. The weather prospects in your area are good. Congratulations. This certainly looks like being a bright weekend for all you fortunate Maidstoneites. The forecast for today *and* tomorrow *and* Monday is bright sunshine and . . . and a party political broadcast on behalf of the Kent County Council and . . .'

Arty banged the tuning key.

'. . . is bright sunshine and sunshine . . . retailing at ninety-five pounds with a discount. . .'

'Give it a kick,' Lance advised. 'Check.'

'. . . a slight breeze from the South West should keep you comfortably cool. Thank you for calling. Have a nice day.'

'There you are,' Arty said. 'It's not raining.'

'I don't trust that thing,' Lance said. 'For all you know, that could be last week's forecast. No one's going to bother to find out, are they? They couldn't prove anything if they did. Look, I said check,' he said to PREM. PREM put out its arm to remedy the situation and jittered backwards under the storage unit.

'What's the point of being the Rose Street Gang if we never play in the street?' Arty complained. 'We might just as well call ourselves the Walkway Mob or the Level Eleveners.'

'And get mistaken for the Level Tenners? Not likely,' Lance said. 'Look, PREM, you're beaten. Why not give up? Anyway,' he went on, 'no one could say it.' He experimented. 'Leveleleveners . . . Leveleleveners . . . it sounds like a tongue-twister.' He reached under the storage unit to winkle out his sulking robot.

'You said we could play in the street when summer came,' Arty persisted.

'I don't feel like it,' Lance said. 'It's too much of a

hassle getting there. Anyway, I'm going down to Beowulf's. He was getting a new hologram for his birthday. D'you want to come?'

'I suppose so. It doesn't look like we're going to do anything else, does it?'

Lance stowed PREM in the storage unit and they headed for the door.

'Where are you off to?' Mum yelled from the utility area, where the laundry module was spewing grey suds across the floor through faulty grommets.

'Just down to Beowulf's.'

'What about lunch?'

'We'll be back for dinner.'

'You'd better take these.' Mum stepped across the spreading puddle of scum and handed him a luncheon module full of anonymous plastic cubes. 'You might as well finish them up,' Mum said. 'The labels have peeled off.' The labels were also in the module, independently advertising the presence of Crunchy Haddock Bites, Crispy Banana Fries, Spicy Nibbles and Flaky Praties. The eatables from which they had disassociated themselves were all uniform six-centimetre blocks.

'You can have a sort of guessing game,' Mum said, encouragingly. 'You won't know which they are until you've tasted them.'

Arty privately thought that without the labels they would not know what they were eating even after they'd eaten it. Sulking as obtrusively as PREM he followed his brother on to the walkway. In fact he had no objection at all to going to see Beowulf's hologram because he had heard, through rumour at the Education Centre, that it was properly not a hologram at all, but one of the new autograms that operated without a plate. He had a hologram of his own, on which you could fight historic battles of the Second World War, but the machine, which had belonged to his father when *he* was a boy, was very nearly as historic as its subject matter, and the Germans kept winning at El Alamein. But at least it still worked.

He and Lance trudged in silence for about twenty minutes along the walkway, past Tesco's, Mothercare, the Education Centre which stretched for hundreds of metres, and the Hydroponic Memorial Facility where Senior Citizens dozed peacefully among the sandbags.

Beowulf lived on the far side of the Hydro in a row of housing units that had gone badly downhill during the previous decade but which were being renovated by artistic people like Beowulf's parents. The artistic nature of Beowulf's parents accounted for his odd name. There were five other Arthurs in the Fourth Year Horizontal Band Module at the Level Eleven Education Centre, and three Lancelots in his Vertical Grouping Unit alone. Thanks to the success of *The Dark Age Saga* which had been running on Network Video for fifteen years, six nights a week with daily repeats at 11.00 and 15.00 hours for shift workers, an omnibus edition on Sundays and continuous showing of early episodes on Channel Seven, there were very few children under the age of fourteen who did not owe their names to the leading characters such as Merlin, Guinever, Gareth, Vivienne and Galahad. Arty knew personally only two: Beowulf Hopkins himself, whose name came from a cult serial on BBC3 and Jason Cropper, whose mum was simply old-fashioned.

Lance pushed the stridulating bell unit by the door frame and from the Private Address module came Beowulf's mum's voice demanding, '*Now* who is it?'

'It's Lance and Arty Cooper, Mrs Hopkins,' Lance said, politely. In Mrs Hopkins's view, he and Arty came from the wrong end of the walkway. Beowulf often remarked cryptically that if she knew what went on at their own end after dark, she might think twice before saying it. Beowulf himself tended to spend his leisure hours lurking round the shafts of the elevation modules, against the chance of an encounter with the Level Tenners. The Rose Street Gang were hoping devoutly for just one encounter with the Level Tenners before the Security Forces descended on them.

The interior of the Hopkinses' flat seemed to change shape every time Arty saw it. Mr Hopkins was a great one for knocking down walls and erecting partitions. Like the Coopers he had cooking areas, eating areas, utility areas, which he referred to quaintly as rooms, and in the middle a huge empty space, with chairs, which he called the *living* room. Why not a dying room too? Arty wondered. When they went in Beowulf was squatting in the centre of the living room in an attitude of irascible dejection, stabbing angrily at a small control module with glowing LEDS.

'Hallo, it's us,' Lance said. 'Where is it, then?'

Beowulf did not look up. 'Where's what, then?' He banged the control module furiously against the side of his knee.

'The autogram.'

'You tell me,' Beowulf snapped. 'In here, I suppose.' He poked the module. 'I can't get the bleeder out. I've only seen him once. He went on the blink as soon as he appeared.'

'Let's have a look,' Lance said, masterfully.

'It's malfunctioning. Looking at it won't help.'

They wrangled over the module. Arty approached the Factcentre and dialled first Adscan, then Retail Leisure Aids, then Autograms. On the screen appeared a moving picture of an autogram which was fairly pointless, Arty thought, as it looked, in the projection, just like an ordinary hologram or even a real person, masquerading as a hologram. This was followed by a list of available models. The autograms were heavily educational and featured Notable People from Living History, and one or two Ordinary People, who were not so educational, such as a cave man, a Roman Soldier, a medieval serf, a Seventeenth-Century Cavalier (get a Roundhead to match: big reduction!), an Eighteenth-Century Hussar with horse (horse extra and indispensable), a Nineteenth-Century Granny and a Twentieth-Century Commando. There history ended.

'Which one have you got?' Arty asked.

'Twentieth-Century Commando, I *suppose*,'

Beowulf said. 'He wasn't around long enough to find out.' He pushed the discarded packaging towards Arty with his foot. 'Captain Courage.'

Arty stooped to pick up the box and at the same moment Lance contrived to press the correct combination of multifunctional keys. In the corner of the room, like a life-sized, out-of-focus reflection, the autogram was seen to materialize. Evidently it was still malfunctioning. It sidled about, one leg shorter than the other and with a curious dent in its hip as if someone had run into it with a right-angled object. It dipped and sashayed unpleasantly.

'What's it meant to do?' Arty asked, shying away as the image lurched too close.

'It's meant to talk for a start,' Beowulf said, snatching back the control module from Lance. He pressed a key. The autogram began to utter in a low-pitched drawl that was entirely unintelligible.

'What's your name?' Arty asked it.

'It should only respond to my voice,' Beowulf said. 'It's personalized. What-is-your-name?' he said to the autogram, enunciating slowly as if speaking to an idiot.

The autogram turned its head. 'Wha-a-a-at?' It developed a nervous tic in its cheek.

'Your name! Your handle – your monicker!' Beowulf shouted. He rattled the control module and the figure jolted into sudden and unattractive clarity.

There was a picture of Captain Courage on the box in Arty's hands. He was lean but muscular beneath his

37

drab combat costume, and hefted a sub-machine gun in his capable hands. His teeth glinted in a dangerous white smile, his eyes were slitted, his jaw clenched askew with menace.

Arty looked from the picture to the real Captain Courage, or rather, to the illusion that purported to be Captain Courage. Captain Courage slitted his eyes, he smiled whitely; not only his jaw but his entire head was askew. He stooped purposefully, gripping the sub-machine gun. 'Kitty-kitty-kitty,' said Captain Courage. 'Nice kitty. Come to Gran.'

There was a considerable silence in the living room after this.

'What's it supposed to say?' Lance asked, finally. Beowulf grabbed the box from Arty and scowled at the data on the back.

'Drop your Kalashnikov or I'll blow you away,' he complained.

'*Who's* a pretty boy, then?' said Captain Courage. His voice had become winsome and fluting. Beowulf lifted the control module and hurled it against the wall in disgust. Captain Courage contracted slightly and warped, as if seen through flawed glass. 'Isn't it a nice day?' he said.

'That's Nineteenth-Century Granny,' Arty said, light dawning. 'They've programmed him with the wrong voice.' It occurred to him that somewhere in the world there must be an autogram of Nineteenth-Century Granny snarling, 'Drop your Kalashnikov or I'll blow you away.'

'What's a Kalashnikov?' he asked.

'Get the whole set and be the envy of your friends!' said Adscan, which had been mumbling to itself in the Factcentre. 'Imagine! A whole cohort of Roman Soldiers !'

'Imagine, a whole cohort of Nineteenth-Century Grannies!' Beowulf mimicked, savagely.

'Lovely weather for the time of year,' Captain Courage observed, from his corner. He bobbed a horrid curtsey as Beowulf picked up the control module from beside his feet where it had rebounded from the plastic wall boarding. He fiddled with the keys and Captain Courage jived wildly, but did not go away.

'It's jammed,' Beowulf said in alarm. 'I can't switch him off.'

'How are your cauliflowers coming along?' Captain Courage inquired.

'What's a cauliflower?' Arty said.

'Damn this for a lark,' Beowulf said. 'I'm going out. You don't catch me stuck here all day with Grandma Courage.'

'What about us?' Lance demanded. 'I told Mum we'd be out till dinner. It's her day at the Conversation Centre. She'll have put the security units on by now and we'll be locked out.'

Arty seized his chance. 'Let's go and play in the street,' he said.

'I don't care where we play,' Beowulf growled. He strode into the cooking area. His mother, who called it a kitchen, was stirring food in a pot over the stove.

She went in for organic cookery. Captain Courage lurched after him.

'We're going out, Mum,' Beowulf said. He put the control module on a shelf and began to tiptoe out of the kitchen.

'Get that thing out of here,' Mrs Hopkins said. 'It gives me the creeps.' Captain Courage leaned at a dangerous angle over the hot plate and writhed hideously in the steam.

'It's a very fine morning,' said Captain Courage.

'He's stuck at "on",' Beowulf said.

'I don't care where he's stuck as long as he's not stuck here,' said Mrs Hopkins. 'I don't know; as soon as you get something you either lose it or break it.'

'I'll leave it in the bedroom.'

'No, you won't. You'll take it with you. I'm not having it hanging around here all day talking to itself.'

'It only responds to my voice,' Beowulf said.

'Take it *with* you.'

The three of them trailed on to the walkway, and the door slammed shut behind them. After a moment Captain Courage followed them out, through the door.

'Are you going to whistle up the others?' Lance asked.

'What others?'

'*Isn't* it a nice day?'

'You shut up,' Beowulf said, over his shoulder.

'The rest of the gang.'

'I don't know that I want anyone to see me while *he's* around,' Beowulf said, jerking his head towards Captain Courage, who jerked back, all over.

'Never mind the others,' Arty said. 'Let's go and play in the street.'

'What's all this with the street?' Beowulf said.

'If you get me the wool, I'll knit one for you.'

'*Will* you belt up?'

'He thinks because we're the Rose Street Gang we ought to go and play in Rose Street,' Lance explained.

'It's three years since I've been in the street,' Arty said. 'I can't hardly remember what it looks like, even.'

'Look,' Beowulf said patiently, to Arty, 'we're the Rose Street Gang because we live in the Rose Street Development. We don't need to go out in the street.'

'Where did I leave my umbrella?'

'The Level Tenners live in the Rose Street Development too,' Arty said, 'but everyone knows that they come from Level Ten. They've got identity.'

'They've got a reputation.'

'What a nice day,' said Captain Courage.

'What price identity?' said Beowulf.

They were passing the Hydroponic Memorial Facility. With a practised and unobtrusive flick of the wrist he spun the control module in among the sandbags. Captain Courage, after a moment's delay, staggered after it and began to float abstractedly between the palm trees murmuring, 'Here, kitty. Kitty-kitty-kitty.'

'Quick, before he notices,' Beowulf said, and started to move away.

'Don't be daft,' Lance said, 'he doesn't know anything;' but he hastily joined Beowulf and Arty who were sauntering down the walkway looking innocent. They were scarcely level with Marks and Spencer before an enraged shout halted them.

'Oi! You lot! Come back here.'

An irate Senior Citizen was advancing with unwonted nimbleness along the walkway, waving the control module above his head. Behind him came Captain Courage, emitting inarticulate squawks.

''Snot mine,' Beowulf said, turning his back. ''Snothing to do with us.'

'I saw you !'

'. . . Cauliauliflowowowers . . .'

'I saw you chuck it in,' the Senior Citizen cried, and lobbed the control module towards them. 'Take it away, Beowulf Hopkins, or I'll tell your dad.'

'That's the trouble with this dump,' Beowulf said, stooping to pick up the module. Captain Courage, who had disintegrated in flight, reassembled himself and glided in their direction. 'Everybody knows everybody else.'

'Lovely weather for the time of year.'

'His feet don't touch the ground any more,' Arty said, as the Captain drifted abreast of them.

'Look,' Lance said, 'we're going to be out all day. Let's drop in at Tesco's and buy some fodder. Mum gave us a load of stuff, but we'll need more, and something to drink.'

Tesco's was a hundred metres long and two metres deep. The boys roved from coin slot to coin slot, purchasing food and cans. As Lance fed in the coins Beowulf lifted the packages from the service apertures beneath. At the last one he took out a six-pack of Coolacola and slipped in the control module.

'Get moving,' he said. They hurried on, leaving Captain Courage in animated conversation with a chewing gum dispenser.

'Well, fancy seeing you! Isn't it a nice day?'

'Are we going to collect the others or not?' Beowulf said as they continued down the walkway.

'Don't look round now,' Lance said. 'We're being followed.'

They all looked round and stopped. A shopping area attendant was steaming up behind, followed by Captain Courage, now inclining several degrees from the perpendicular and chatting vivaciously with a rat which was running along the gap where the wall had subsided away from the ceiling.

'I saw you,' the shopping area attendant said. 'It's an offence, depositing foreign articles in the service apertures. It's an offence, that is. I could get you had up for that.'

Wordlessly Beowulf received the control module and they resumed their journey.

'Let's go down to Level Ten at least,' Arty said.

'There's a thought,' said Lance. 'Perhaps we could

leave him in the lift,' but when they reached the elevation unit area a large and partially illuminated sign informed them: ELEVATION UNITS TEMPORARILY OUT OF ACTION. DANGER. MEN AT WORK.

There were no men at work.

'Can't we drop it down one of the shafts?' Lance said.

'We'll never get near,' Beowulf said. 'They'll have the deterrent beams switched on.'

'If you get me the wool, I'll knit one for you.'

'I don't suppose they'll be working either,' Lance said, advancing hopefully towards the open shafts. 'Ouch! They are, though.'

'We'll have to use the stairs,' Arty said. 'We might meet the Level Tenners. Let's get the others, Lance. *Let's.*'

'If we can find a telecom that's not US,' Lance said. 'Where's the nearest?'

They walked on for another fifteen minutes towards the stairs and the telecom units that stood in a vandal-proof line against the wall. Most of them had been torn from their mountings.

'Got any money?' Beowulf asked.

'People like you ought to be locked up,' Captain Courage rebuked him, severely.

'A fiver.' Lance took out the coin and pressed it into the one slot that was not already plugged with super glue, super gum or Spicy Nibbles.

'Hello?' he said. 'Hello!' he shouted, into the sticky mouthpiece. 'Is that you, Kay?'

'You don't have to shout,' said Kay Lambert, a block and a half away.

Lance said, 'Look, Kay, we're going down a few levels –' Arty pricked up his ears, '– and the lifts are US. We may need reinforcements. Interested?'

Kay's voice became thick and grainy at this point, but Lance understood him to say that he'd be there.

'Bring the others,' Lance said. 'We'll meet you at the head of the North Stairs. Half an hour? OK?' The line went dead. He replaced the oral module. 'That should just give us time to get there,' he said, 'if we start walking now.'

They started walking. Captain Courage followed, a few paces behind, veering and backing crazily upon his own axis.

'When we get to the next corner,' Beowulf promised, 'we'll lose him.'

'My mum'd go spare if I lost something like that,' Lance said. 'They cost about three thousand each.'

'Three thousand, seven hundred and fifty, that one,' Beowulf said. 'My mum'll go spare too, but she'll be even sparer if I take this loony back again.'

'Perhaps your dad can mend him,' Arty said. 'He's good with his hands.'

'He'd need to be good with a hammer,' Beowulf said, 'to get anywhere with *him*.'

'He's quite good fun, really,' Arty said, wistfully. It was almost like having a mad but harmless adult in tow, and if they were going down to the lower levels an adult, even a mad and harmless one, could be nothing but an asset on those shadowy walkways below.

Beowulf shoved the control module into his hands. '*You* look after him then, if you think so much of him. If anyone asks, he's yours.' He stalked ahead, with Lance, and Arty trailed behind, experimentally depressing various keys. He felt that Beowulf simply did not understand Captain Courage. If you pressed *Volume Control* the Captain rose to shoulder height. *Forward Motion* made him reach for his gun and *Lateral Hold* made him fling himself defensively to the ground. In spite of curious looks from passers-by, Arty kept his fingers on *Volume Control* and *Lateral Hold*, and the Captain swam alongside him, tossing off comments in response to Beowulf's distant remarks to Lance.

'Isn't it a nice day?' 'If you get me the wool, I'll make one for you.' 'How are your cauliflowers coming along?'

'What's a cauliflower?' Arty asked, but neither of the others answered.

'Where *did* I leave my umbrella?'

'What's an umbrella?' said Arty. 'What's wool?'

Harrison Bergeron

KURT VONNEGUT

Kurt Vonnegut, an American, uses a
typewriter as if it were a slashing knife. His
writing is fast, ferocious, tricky, sardonic, very
funny and very disturbing. First acclaimed in
the 1950s (a 'golden age' of SF) he refused to
be labelled as a science fiction writer; everyday
realities were the only launching pad needed
for flights of fantasy.

The year was 2081, and everybody was finally
equal. They weren't only equal before God and
the law, they were equal every which way. Nobody
was smarter than anybody else; nobody was better
than anybody else; nobody was stronger or quicker
than anybody else. All this equality was due to the
211th, 212th and 213th Amendments to the Constitu-
tion, and to the unceasing vigilance of agents of the
United States Handicapper-General.

Some things about living still weren't quite right,

48

though. April, for instance, still drove people crazy by not being springtime. And it was in that clammy month that the H-G men took George and Hazel Bergeron's fourteen-year-old son Harrison away.

It was tragic, all right, but George and Hazel couldn't think about it very hard. Hazel had a perfectly average intelligence, which meant she couldn't think about anything except in short bursts. And George, while his intelligence was way above normal, had a little mental-handicap radio in his ear – he was required by law to wear it at all times. It was tuned to a government transmitter and, every twenty seconds or so, the transmitter would send out some sharp noise to keep people like George from taking unfair advantage of their brains.

George and Hazel were watching television. There were tears on Hazel's cheeks, but she'd forgotten for the moment what they were about, as the ballerinas came to the end of a dance.

A buzzer sounded in George's head. His thoughts fled in panic, like bandits from a burglar alarm.

'That was a real pretty dance, that dance they just did,' said Hazel.

'Huh?' said George.

'That dance – it was nice,' said Hazel.

'Yup,' said George. He tried to think a little about the ballerinas. They weren't really very good – no better than anybody else would have been, anyway. They were burdened with sashweights and bags of birdshot, and their faces were masked, so that no one, seeing a free and graceful gesture or a pretty face, would feel like something the cat dragged in. George was toying with the vague notion that maybe dancers shouldn't be handicapped. But he didn't get very far with it before another noise in his ear radio scattered his thoughts.

George winced. So did two out of the eight ballerinas.

Hazel saw him wince. Having no mental handicap herself, she had to ask George what the latest sound had been.

'Sounded like somebody hitting a milk bottle with a ballpeen hammer,' said George.

'I'd think it would be real interesting, hearing all the different sounds,' said Hazel, a little envious. 'The things they think up.'

'Um,' said George.

'Only, if I was Handicapper-General, you know what I would do?' said Hazel. Hazel, as a matter of fact, bore a strong resemblance to the Handicapper-General, a woman named Diana Moon Glampers. 'If I was Diana Moon Glampers,' said Hazel, 'I'd have chimes on Sunday – just chimes. Kind of in honour of religion.'

'I could think, if it was just chimes,' said George.

'Well – maybe make 'em real loud,' said Hazel. 'I think I'd make a good Handicapper-General.'

'Good as anybody else,' said George.

'Who knows better'n I do what normal is?' said Hazel.

'Right,' said George. He began to think glimmer-ingly about his abnormal son who was now in jail, about Harrison, but a twenty-one-gun salute in his head stopped that.

'Boy!' said Hazel, 'that was a doozy, wasn't it?'

It was such a doozy that George was white and trembling, and tears stood on the rims of his red eyes. Two of the eight ballerinas had collapsed to the studio floor, and were holding their temples.

'All of a sudden you look so tired,' said Hazel. 'Why don't you stretch out on the sofa, so's you can rest your handicap bag on the pillows, honeybunch.' She was referring to the forty-seven pounds of birdshot in a canvas bag, which was padlocked around George's neck. 'Go on and rest the bag for a little while,' she said. 'I don't care if you're not equal to me for a while.'

George weighed the bag with his hands. 'I don't mind it,' he said. 'I don't notice it anymore. It's just a part of me.'

'You been so tired lately – kind of wore out,' said Hazel. 'If there was just some way we could make a little hole in the bottom of the bag, and just take out a few of them lead balls. Just a few.'

'Two years in prison and two thousand dollars fine for every ball took out,' said George. 'I don't call that a bargain.'

'If you could just take a few out when you came home from work,' said Hazel. 'I mean – you don't compete with anybody around here. You just set around.'

'If I tried to get away with it,' said George, 'then

other people'd get away with it – and pretty soon we'd be right back to the dark ages again, with everybody competing against everybody else. You wouldn't like that, would you?'

'I'd hate it,' said Hazel.

'There you are,' said George. 'The minute people start cheating on laws, what do you think happens to society?'

If Hazel hadn't been able to come up with an answer to this question, George couldn't have supplied one. A siren was going off in his head.

'Reckon it'd fall all apart,' said Hazel.

'What would?' said George blankly.

'Society,' said Hazel uncertainly. 'Wasn't that what you just said?'

'Who knows?' said George.

The television programme was suddenly interrupted for a news bulletin. It wasn't clear at first as to what the bulletin was about, since the announcer, like all announcers, had a serious speech impediment. For about half a minute, and in a state of high excitement, the announcer tried to say, 'Ladies and gentlemen –'

He finally gave up, handed the bulletin to a ballerina to read.

'That's all right,' Hazel said of the announcer, 'he tried. That's the big thing. He tried to do the best he could with what God gave him. He should get a nice raise for trying so hard.'

'Ladies and gentlemen –' said the ballerina, reading the bulletin. She must have been extraordinarily beautiful, because the mask she wore was hideous. And it was easy to see that she was the strongest and most graceful of all the dancers, for her handicap bags were as big as those worn by 200-pound men.

And she had to apologize at once for her voice, which was a very unfair voice for a woman to use. Her voice was a warm, luminous, timeless melody. 'Excuse me –' she said, and she began again, making her voice absolutely uncompetitive.

'Harrison Bergeron, age fourteen,' she said in a grackle squawk, 'has just escaped from gaol, where he was held on suspicion of plotting to overthrow the government. He is a genius and an athlete, is under-handicapped, and is extremely dangerous.'

A police photograph of Harrison Bergeron was flashed on the screen – upside down, then sideways, upside down again, then right-side up. The picture showed the full length of Harrison against a back-ground calibrated in feet and inches. He was exactly seven feet tall.

The rest of Harrison's appearance was Hallowe'en and hardware. Nobody had ever borne heavier handi-caps. He had outgrown hindrances faster than the H–G men could think them up. Instead of a little ear-radio for a mental handicap, he wore a tremendous pair of earphones, and spectacles with thick, wavy lenses besides. The spectacles were intended not only to make him half-blind, but to give him whanging headaches as well.

Scrap metal was hung all over him. Ordinarily, there was a certain symmetry, a military neatness to the handicaps issued to strong people, but Harrison looked like a walking junkyard. In the race of life, Harrison carried 300 pounds.

And, to offset his good looks, the H–G men required that he wear at all times a red rubber ball for a nose, keep his eyebrows shaved off, and cover his even white teeth with black caps at snaggle-tooth random.

'If you see this boy,' said the ballerina, 'do not – I repeat, do not – try to reason with him.'

There was the shriek of a door being torn from its hinges.

Screams and barking cries of consternation came from the television set. The photograph of Harrison Bergeron on the screen jumped again and again, as though dancing to the tune of an earthquake.

George Bergeron correctly identified the earthquake, and he might have – for many was the time his own home had danced to the same crashing tune. 'My God!' said George. 'That must be Harrison!'

The realization was blasted from his mind instantly by the sound of an automobile collision in his head.

When George could open his eyes again, the photograph of Harrison was gone. A living, breathing Harrison filled the screen.

Clanking, clownish and huge, Harrison stood in the centre of the studio. The knob of the uprooted studio-door was still in his hand. Ballerinas, technicians, musicians and announcers cowered on their knees before him, expecting to die.

'I am the Emperor!' cried Harrison. 'Do you hear? I

am the Emperor! Everybody must do what I say at once!' He stamped his foot and the studio shook.

'Even as I stand here,' he bellowed, 'crippled, hobbled, sickened, I am a greater ruler than any man who ever lived! Now watch me become what I *can* become!'

Harrison tore the straps of his handicap harness like wet tissue-paper, tore straps guaranteed to support 5000 pounds.

Harrison's scrap-iron handicaps crashed to the floor.

Harrison thrust his thumbs under the bar of the padlock that secured his head harness. The bar snapped like celery. Harrison smashed his headphones and spectacles against the wall.

He flung away his rubber-ball nose, revealed a man that would have awed Thor, the god of thunder.

'I shall now select my Empress!' he said, looking down on the cowering people. 'Let the first woman who dares rise to her feet claim her mate and her throne!'

A moment passed, and then a ballerina arose, swaying like a willow.

Harrison plucked the mental handicap from her ear, snapped off her physical handicaps with marvellous delicacy. Last of all, he removed her mask.

She was blindingly beautiful.

'Now –' said Harrison, taking her hand. 'Shall we show the people the meaning of the word "dance"? Music!' he commanded.

The musicians scrambled back into their chairs, and Harrison stripped them of their handicaps, too. 'Play your best,' he told them, 'and I'll make you barons and dukes and earls.'

The music began. It was normal at first — cheap, silly, false. But Harrison snatched two musicians from their chairs, waved them like batons as he sang the music as he wanted it played. He slammed them back into their chairs.

The music began again, and was much improved.

Harrison and his Empress merely listened to the music for a while – listened gravely, as though synchronizing their heartbeats with it.

They shifted their weight to their toes.

Harrison placed his big hands on the girl's tiny waist, letting her sense the weightlessness that would soon be hers.

And then, in an explosion of joy and grace, into the air they sprang!

Not only were the laws of the land abandoned, but the law of gravity and the laws of motion as well.

They reeled, whirled, swivelled, flounced, capered, gambolled and spun.

They leaped like deer on the moon.

The studio ceiling was thirty feet high, but each leap brought the dancers nearer to it.

It became their obvious intention to kiss the ceiling.

They kissed it.

And then, neutralizing gravity with love and pure will, they remained suspended in air inches below the ceiling, and they kissed each other for a long, long time.

It was then that Diana Moon Glampers, the

Handicapper-General, came into the studio with a double-barrelled ten-gauge shotgun. She fired twice, and the Emperor and the Empress were dead before they hit the floor.

Diana Moon Glampers loaded the gun again. She aimed it at the musicians and told them they had ten seconds to get their handicaps back on.

It was then that the Bergerons' television tube burned out.

Hazel turned to comment about the blackout to George. But George had gone out into the kitchen for a can of beer.

George came back in with the beer, paused while a handicap signal shook him up. And then he sat down again. 'You been crying?' he said to Hazel, watching her wipe her tears.

'Yup,' she said.

'What about?' he said.

'I forget,' she said. 'Something real sad on television.'

'What was it?' he said.

'It's all kind of mixed up in my mind,' said Hazel.

'Forget sad things,' said George.

'I always do,' said Hazel.

'That's my girl,' said George. He winced. There was the sound of a riveting-gun in his head.

'Gee – I could tell that one was a doozy,' said Hazel.

'You can say that again,' said George.

'Gee –' said Hazel. 'I could tell that one was a doozy.'

Confluence

BRIAN ALDISS

Hi-fi, High-tech, microchip, trainers, VIP, rock and roll: we had to invent these terms. What new words may be needed in other worlds and other times?

Confluence is the language of Myrin, a planet some eleven million years old. The meaning of Confluent words can be changed by the posture and action of the speaker. (Much the same is true of written Chinese: the calligrapher can write the same character offensively or flatteringly.) Brian Aldiss was a prime mover of the 1970s British 'New Wave' in SF. He explored fresher, subtler possibilities. Here is a sprinkling of Confluence words and phrases . . .

AB W TEL MIN: The sensation that one neither agrees nor disagrees with what is being said to one, but that one simply wishes to depart from the presence of the speaker.

CHAM ON TH ZAM: Being witty when nobody else appreciates it.

HE YUP: The first words the computers spoke, meaning 'The light will not be necessary'.

JILY JIP TUP: A thinking machine that develops a stammer; the action of pulling up trousers while running uphill.

LAHAH SIP: Tasting fresh air after one has worked several hours at one's desk.

MAL: A feeling of being watched from within.

SHAK ALE MAN: The struggle that takes place in the night between the urge to urinate and the urge to continue sleeping.

SHE EAN MIK: Performing prohibited postures before a mirror.

STAIN TOK I: The awareness that one is helplessly living a role.

YUP PA: A book in which everything is understandable except the author's purpose in writing it.

Very well, then: there are some of the things the Confluence language can convey. Would you like to take the idea further? Do you need words to express, say, 'The sick realization that you have not brought to school the very book or piece of work that will be demanded'? Or, 'The joyful realization that, after all you will not actually have to fight the person you challenged?' Or, 'The necessity of hiding, from the person who has brought a much better lunch than yours, your envy'?

Of Polymuf Stock

JOHN CHRISTOPHER

John Christopher is one of the pioneer British
SF writers who, in the 1950s forced their way
into what had previously been a virtually all-
American cult market. His *The Death of Grass*
was an early international hit. He followed
with a succession of short and long works of
great distinction, including *The White
Mountain*, *The City of Gold* and *The Pool of
Fire* – all for young readers. You may
remember the British TV serializations: *The
Tripods*, the 'capping' of the boys . . .

Oh – the word 'polymuf': take it to mean
'polymorphous' – many-shaped.

I was born true man, but of polymuf stock.
Until I was nine I knew nothing of this. I was the
son of Andrew Harding, chief of the Captains. I had
an elder brother and two elder sisters, and lived in the

Harding house which looked proudly at the palace from across the square. I had a nurse and servants to do my bidding.

One day, having quarrelled with a friend, I found myself alone in a part of the city, near the East Gate, I had rarely visited. The streets were mean, the houses pinched and crowded, and there were smells that made me wrinkle my nose. A dead cat in the gutter must have been there a week.

In one rotting street three boys followed me. Their tunics were of cheap cloth and both their clothes and they would have been better for washing. They jeered at me; then came past and planted themselves in my path. One demanded my name and I told him: Harding. It proved they were Blainites.

The Hardings and the Blaines had been rivals for generations. This was normally concealed under a show of politeness but at a lower level, among their followers, the feud was open. The three young Blainites were delighted to find a solitary Harding in their territory. They would not have dared touch me, since I was noble, but taunts leave no traces. In the end it was I who turned violent, launching myself at my chief tormentor, who happened to be the biggest.

Had things been equal I would have been no match for him, because he was used to rough fighting. But he was held back by awareness of my rank, and probably by the thought of retribution. I had no such scruples and was rubbing his face in the dirt when we were pulled apart and lifted to our feet. A crowd had collected.

Questions were asked, my name required again. One man said:

'Isak! The one who . . .'

His voice dropped to a whisper I could not catch. I heard other whispers and saw glances exchanged. It meant nothing at the time except that they were Blainites. I noticed with satisfaction that my recent opponent was crying, and turned away. I had gone several paces when a voice called:

'Polymuf! The Harding polymuf brat.'

That meant nothing either, being plain nonsense. I knew I bore no malformation of the body. I walked on, towards the city centre. Boys followed, chanting:

'Polymuf . . . polymuf!'

It was some stupidity the Blainites had devised to insult their betters. I came into Bird Street where troopers were comparing notes on caged finches, and the boys fell back and left me.

A few days later, I heard the jeer repeated in the street. I still did not think it mattered or I would not have spoken casually of it to David Greene. He knew nothing either, but he asked, and was told, and told me.

Every child born had to be taken to the Seer, to be scrutinized for defects of the body. Those with none were classed as true men, the short-legged ones as dwarfs. The rest, even where the defect was no more than a missing finger, were polymufs, who must serve true men who had no rights and could hold no property.

A rejected child of human stock was given to a dwarf or polymuf foster-mother for rearing. The reverse was also true. And this, David said, had been my case. I had been brought to the Seance Hall by polymuf parents, judged true man by the Seer, and given to the Hardings.

I listened in disbelieving horror. David's eyes watched me. He was not smiling but I read the smile behind them, and more: pity, contempt. I said:

'That's a lie!'

He shrugged. 'Perhaps. It is what they say.'

I made an excuse to leave him, and ran home. It was a cold grey morning, threatening rain. The doorman rose from his stool to salute me, heaving up his twisted body.

My nurse Betty was in my room. The housemaids had cleaned it, but she must always do a final setting to rights. As long as I could remember I had taken questions to her for answering, troubles for soothing. But when she looked at me from her single eye, I could not speak. From infancy the deformity had meant nothing, but now I turned and ran. She called but I paid no heed.

I ran across the courtyard, heading for the stables. As I reached them, I collided with someone coming out. I was checked and held. My father's voice said:

'What haste, boy?' I looked up, but could not speak.

'And tears? A Harding does not cry, when he is nine years old.'

I said, gasping: 'A Harding, sir? Or a polymuf's brat?'

He stared at me, his face closed and seeming hard. I thought he might strike me, and almost welcomed it. But he said:

'We have talking to do, Isak. Come.'

He was not a tall man, and sparely built. His face too was thin, with keen blue eyes and a well trimmed beard, turning white. It had never occurred to me to look for a resemblance to my own heavy features in his. I did so now, then turned my head away.

We sat in his business room, with the parchment rent rolls hanging on sticks on the wall and logs crackling noisily in the hearth. He was a man who felt the cold and sought warmth where he could. He sat in his chair, covered with the chestnut hide of a favourite horse that had been killed under him in battle, I on a leather stool before him.

'The tears have stopped,' he said. 'Good. Now, tell me what you have heard.'

I would have broken down in the telling except that his unblinking eyes forbade it. When I had finished, I asked:

'Is it true, sir?'

He nodded. 'As far as it goes.'

I began to sob, and he put a hand on my shoulder.

'A Harding does not cry.'

'But I am none!'

'You are.'

'I am not your son.'

'No,' he said. 'But of my line and blood. You are my grandson, Isak.'

I stared, uncomprehending. He said:

'My first-born child was a girl. The Seer named her polymuf and she was taken from us. It is the law, and the Spirits command it. My wife grieved deeply and died within two winters. Later I married again and my children were whole and human. These you have called your sisters and your brother.'

He paused, and I waited. 'Years later the Seer came to me. A polymuf woman had borne a boy who was true man and must be given to true men for rearing. The woman was my daughter. My wife and I took you. You are my own, a Harding.'

'My mother . . .'

'Has doubtless had other children.'

'Who is she? Where does she live?'

He shook his head. 'We do not know.'

'But . . .'

'It is the law, Isak. The Seer knows, but no other may. I was not informed as to whom she was given, nor she that you were given back to me. The Seer told me of your ancestry because it seemed fitting to him. And I . . .' He paused again. 'I thanked him, and the Spirits, and made an offering which he called generous. It was a poor return for what I had been given.'

'And my true father?'

'Who knows?'

Who knew, indeed? I thought of polymuf men I had passed unthinkingly, with all the diversity of ugliness the evil Spirits might wreak on an unborn child. I thought of Grog, who used four arms in sweeping the street, and Petey, who had a double row of teeth which he displayed for the troopers who bought him ale. Any one might have been my father.

'And it does not matter,' my grandfather said. I stared at him, hot-eyed. 'You are a Harding. Those who have dared mock you will regret it.'

I never knew what word went out, but there were no more cries of 'Polymuf'. The Hardings, as I have said, were powerful. My grandfather, having bidden me forget what I had learnt, made sure none reminded me of it. But there was no need of reminder. The truth sank deep and lay with the cold weight of iron. Polymufs became monstrous to me, even Betty. I flinched from her touch and the gaze of her single eye.

It was customary for a boy of noble family to leave home at eleven for a spell in the barracks. I begged to go when I was ten, and this was granted. When I returned it was with high praise from the Drill Sergeant. I showed great promise: he had rarely known a boy so eager to excel.

The fact was that I loved the barracks, a place where no polymuf was permitted entry. I grew drunk with the smell of horses and leather, the clash of swords and the jingle of harness irons. The hardships of the life exalted me. They were trials for true men.

I made no friends and wanted none. The other boys talked, I guessed, behind my back – maybe called me polymuf when I was out of hearing. But they watched their words in my company. I did not mind if they liked or disliked me. It was enough that they dropped their eyes before mine.

The later years of my childhood passed during a time in which great events took place. Prince Stephen was deposed, and replaced by Robert Perry. Intrigue and murder followed and within two years Robert's son Peter was Prince, and his younger son taken to live with the High Seers in Sanctuary. Subsequently Luke returned, and fought and killed his brother, and became Prince, our third within three years. And the following spring, being thirteen, I was named to fight in the Contest.

In this yearly tournament, four sons of Captains led teams of four, which were eliminated in turn as their Captains were unhorsed. The swords were wooden, but they could hurt. It was no sport for weaklings.

My first requirement was to find the best men for my team. My reputation helped. I was known as the best swordsman and one of the two best horsemen of my year; and the followers of the winning Captain would receive gold. To those I canvassed I promised a double sum, relying on my grandfather's pride to make good the promise. Then I drilled them, relentlessly.

Finally I made alliances. It often happened that two Young Captains would agree to fight together first, to eliminate a third. Robin Becket, my chief rival, offered such an arrangement. I accepted, but found excuse not to seal it with a handshake. Then I went to Peter Gray, whose team was reckoned third in strength, and made a bargain for the first round, and this time sealed it.

Robin was confused and shaken when Peter and I rode against him, and put up little opposition. It took less than five minutes' fighting to bring his fall, and the first interval. When the fight resumed I set my men at Peter and here again had the advantage of surprise: our agreement had been for the first round but he had assumed we would keep our alliance to eliminate the fourth Captain, Ranald. Ranald gladly joined us in attacking Peter: to survive into the final round was more honour than he could have hoped for.

Peter fought hard, and three of Ranald's men went down before my sword got him under the ribs and dropped him from his saddle. We waited calmly for the third bell, drove Ranald quickly into a corner, and overthrew him.

It was the shortest Contest in memory, the first for many years in which a team had won without losing a man. As I led my pony to the Prince's pavilion, cheers echoed against the bright sky and bushy top of Catherine's Hill. No one shouted 'Polymuf'. Prince Luke, only a few years older than myself, preferred the hilt of the jewelled sword, which was the victor's prize. He said:

'You fight well, Isak.'

'Thank you, sire.'

'But hard. The surgeon says Peter has a broken rib from that last thrust of yours.'

'Must one not fight hard in battle, sire?'

'In battle, yes.'

He looked as though he might say more, but did not. I lifted the sword to salute him, and the crowd howled louder still.

My victory was not popular among my peers. It was whispered that Robin, feeling cheated, would challenge me to a duel. When I heard that, I sought him out where he sat with friends on the steps of the Buttercross. I stood and looked at him, and he looked away.

I had grown accustomed to my own company and it contented me. Sometimes at night I stood on the city wall, looking down the Itchen valley, and thought of the future. It was through arms that a man achieved glory, but wealth set the seal on success. My grandfather had been a notable warrior, but he owed his position in the city to the prosperity of his farms. Soldiering was not an end but a means. In war one stood to gain booty, and the better one fought the more one got. I vowed I would earn a lion's share. Gregory was my father's elder son and heir, but the day would come when my riches outranked his.

Wealth signified power also. Men had believed no commoner could rise to be Prince, but the Perrys had given the lie to that. They would say it was unthinkable that someone born of polymuf stock could reign. But it was not unthinkable, for I thought it.

I toughened body and mind for the task I had set myself. In the city streets I walked alone and others gave me room. I scarcely saw them. The ones I did notice were the polymufs. That one, the spindly giant nearly eight feet tall: was he my father? And the stooping woman, with a cloth pulled across to hide her face: was she my mother?

On my first campaign I was a scout only, but it made a start. We rode against Romsey, whose army marshalled on the far bank of the river on which the city stood; then edged south along the valley, our army shadowing them across the water. Two days passed in this fashion. It was something that the weather held fair: cloudy, but warm and dry.

On the second night I was given a post on the southern flank, on high ground from which, at dawn, I might spy the Romsey outriders. As evening faded into night the sky emptied of cloud and the air grew calm. White mist rose from the river and spread out.

It reached me in the small hours, a chill miasma that stung throat and eyes. That was a long watch. The mist stifled the small sounds of the night – the owl's cry, the swish of grass or crackle of thicket at an animal's passing. At last, very slowly, the blackness turned to grey, the grey to pearl. But no more than that. I could distinguish a brightness in the east, but the fingers on my outstretched hand were shadowy. I could scarcely see my feet.

I could do no good here, and the mist might last all day, so I decided to rejoin the army. I could not see my way, though, and a scout does not call for help. It was, I thought, a simple matter of heading downhill till I reached the river, then turning right. But the slope did not run continually downwards. There was an intervening ridge and there, unable to see beyond a foot or two ahead, I must have turned south instead of west.

Eventually I knew I was lost. But the mist seemed to be thinning: the brighter pearl of the east was tinged with fitful yellow and at last with gold. A pale disk came and went. Then clear sun, and mist lifting all round.

I was surrounded by rabbit-cropped grass patched with scrub. I could see nothing of the river, but a thorned mound offered a vantage point. Loose bricks underfoot told me this was a ruin from days before the Disaster. Simple people thought such places the haunts of evil Spirits, bound there by the perdition into which they had led mankind, and shunned them. That did not trouble me. Even when the slope collapsed beneath my feet and I found myself falling, I did not think of Spirits – merely cursed my foolishness in not taking more care.

I landed painfully but broke no bones. A jagged

hole, high up, gave little light. I felt in my pack for tinder-box and candle.

I had crashed into a room which apart from the rubble that had fallen with me was untouched. I saw a table and a sideboard, holding objects covered with dust. As I went near, wax from my candle melted and dropped, burning a hole in spider webs and revealing a yellow gleam beneath.

I looked more closely. Pots and plates, salvers, jugs, vases . . . some gold, the rest, though tarnished, plainly silver. I discovered a wide silver dish worked in delicate patterns, and a heavy chain of gold. There were cupboards beneath the sideboard, holding more treasure: a large silver bowl was heaped with smaller ones.

Here was greater booty than a warrior might hope to gain in a score of campaigns, undisturbed for more than a hundred years. It had no owner but the Spirits, and they could have little use for it. I was rich – richer maybe than my grandfather Harding.

Caution succeeded excitement. Even if I could carry all this away, it would be unwise to try. I must take no more than a pot or two. But I could mark the place, and come back whenever I wished and get what I needed. This was barren land, close to one of the great ruins. No one would willingly venture near.

I took a small gold pot and plate, and put them in my pack. When I was older . . . Gold would buy not only houses, farms, servants, but also men. I would have more followers than the Blaines and Hardings put together. And buying men bought power; power enough to take the city, and other cities.

There was a door beyond the table which opened easily. On the far side were buckets, made of that substance called plast, which countrymen, when they turn it up in digging, are careful to burn, washing their hands afterwards. A blue bucket and two yellow ones were heaped with bracelets, brooches and other jewellery of gold set with precious stones. This was not just riches, but wealth incalculable.

I looked further, and saw more: a wooden chest, laden with jewels, a long string of pearls spilling over the edge . . . and a bed, where a figure lay.

He was dead, but I felt no fear of that either. I expected to see the gleam of bone, but flesh still covered him – dried dark, drawn tight from grinning teeth and blackened eyeholes, but preserved. He had died in a dry summer, perhaps, and his flesh had withered instead of rotting. It sometimes happens.

Any such relic of a face would look mean and pinched, but I wondered if his features had in fact changed so much. It was he who had brought the treasure to this spot. When the Disaster struck, and great cities tumbled like play bricks, survivors had fled into the country for safety. But he had gone back into the ruins, risking earthquake and plague, to dig for gold. They had been a rich people, our ancestors, and there had been much to find. He had carried it here, load upon load. A dozen trinkets lay on the bed beside him, like the toys a child puts by its pillow. On his bony wrist were three small clocks, secured by gold bracelets.

How long had he lived here? For years, certainly —
such a hoard could not have been amassed in less time.
And how died? Of sickness, or old age? Or perhaps of
hunger, with no food in reach and unwilling to leave
his treasure to search for it.

In the Disaster the world had been shattered into
ugly fragments, people had died in numbers none
could imagine; and he had huddled here, counting his
wealth by candlelight. He had withered away until
death came, then withered further. He had altered
scarcely more than his changeless gold. Even the rats
had shunned him.

Now at last fear came to me, though it had nothing
to do either with corpse or Spirits. It was rather a
misery that struck deep, a feeling of hopelessness biting
into heart and bones. I had a desperate need to leave
this place, not because of its ghosts but because it held
none — nothing but emptiness and desolation, and
barren treasure.

I went back to the other room. The hole in the
ceiling was out of reach, but with the table upended . . .
I dragged it from the wall, sending its cobwebbed cargo
clattering to the ground, and scrambled on top. Would
the broken laths take my weight? I leapt, felt the edge
give, but clawed my way up to reach a beam. Straddling
it, with the way open to the sky and the world outside, I
felt in my pack for the golden pot and plate, pitched
them down and heard them crash in the darkness.

★

The day was bright, with no more than a white steam coming up from the ground, the sky clear except for wispy cloud. I found the river, and followed it north. Ten minutes later I reached a village, and hurried towards it, joyful at the sound of a dog's bark, the sight of smoking chimneys. At the outskirts a man drew water from a well. He wore servant's clothes, and as he turned I saw one eye had a cast and his right arm was crooked.

He bowed his head. 'Greetings, master.'

I looked at him, and did not shrink away.

I said: 'Greetings, brother.'

From *Kai Lung Unrolls His Mat*

ERNEST BRAMAH

Ernest Bramah's writing and humour were delicate – precise – jewelled like a fine watch. Why is he forgotten?
What supports our world? Why does it not fly off into space? Ah-Shoo, a philosopher, discusses the matter with his son Wan . . .
. . . contrasting the system of Ka-ping, who maintained that the world was suspended from a powerful fibrous rope, with that of Tai-u, who contended that it was supported upon a substantial bamboo pole.

With the clear insight of an original and discerning mind, Ah-Shoo had already detected the fundamental weakness of both theories.

'If the world was indeed dependent on the flexible

retention of an unstable cord, it is inevitable that during the season of Much Wind it must from time to time have been blown into a reversed position, with the distressing result that what was East when we composed ourselves to sleep would be West when we awoke from our slumber, to the confusion of all ordinary process of observation and the well-grounded annoyance of those who, being engaged upon a journey, found themselves compelled to return, and set out again in the opposite direction . . .'

And the bamboo pole theory?

'. . . when the ground became dry and crumbling, the upper end of the pole would enlarge the socket in which it was embedded . . . Even more disturbing would be the outcome of a season of continuous flood, such as our agreeable land frequently enjoys . . . The pole would continue to sink deeper and deeper into the mass, until at length it would protrude upon the upper side, when the earth, deprived of all support, would slide down the pole until it plunged into the impenetrable gloom of the Beneath Parts . . .'

From *The Holy Bible*

THE NEW TESTAMENT:
REVELATIONS 20:1–4; 21:7, 8.

Will we be judged after death? How? By whom?

'Then I saw an angel coming down from heaven, holding in his hand the key of the bottomless pit and a great chain.

'And he seized the dragon, that ancient serpent, who is the Devil and Satan, and bound him for a thousand years, and threw him into the pit, and shut it and sealed it over him . . .'

But, wait: that is the fate awaiting Satan. What of us?

'He who conquers shall have this heritage . . . But the fearful, and unbelieving, and the abominable, and the murderers, and whoremongers, and sorcerers, and idolators, and all liars, shall have their part in the lake that burns with fire and brimstone, which is the second death.'

The Nine Billion Names of God

ARTHUR C CLARKE

It is reported that during World War Two, Clarke and his necessarily few friends of similar intellectual capacity met in a pub to sketch designs for the spaceships of the future. The point of this story is, that the designs proved exactly right.

Clarke puts hard-minded science as well as soaring fantasy into his works. He is highly regarded, widely published. A Britisher, he lived for many years in what was then Ceylon – an ideal place for his telescope observations.

'This is a slightly unusual request,' said Dr Wagner, with what he hoped was commendable restraint. 'As far as I know, it's the first time anyone's been asked to supply a Tibetan monastery with an

Automatic Sequence Computer. I don't wish to be inquisitive, but I should hardly have thought that your – ah – establishment had much use for such a machine. Could you explain just what you intend to do with it?'

'Gladly,' replied the lama, readjusting his silk robes and carefully putting away the slide rule he had been using for currency conversions. 'Your Mark V Computer can carry out any routine mathematical operation involving up to ten digits. However, for our work we are interested in *letters*, not numbers. As we wish you to modify the output circuits, the machine will be printing words, not columns of figures.'

'I don't quite understand . . .'

'This is a project on which we have been working for the last three centuries – since the lamasery was founded, in fact. It is somewhat alien to your way of thought, so I hope you will listen with an open mind while I explain it.'

'Naturally.'

'It is really quite simple. We have been compiling a list which shall contain all the possible names of God.'

'I beg your pardon?'

'We have reason to believe,' continued the lama imperturbably, 'that all such names can be written with not more than nine letters in an alphabet we have devised.'

'And you have been doing this for three centuries?'

'Yes: we expected it would take us about fifteen thousand years to complete the task.'

'Oh,' Dr Wagner looked a little dazed. 'Now I see why you wanted to hire one of our machines. But what exactly is the purpose of this project?'

The lama hesitated for a fraction of a second, and Wagner wondered if he had offended him. If so, there was no trace of annoyance in the reply.

'Call it ritual, if you like, but it's a fundamental part of our belief. All the many names of the Supreme Being – God, Jehova, Allah, and so on – they are only man-made labels. There is a philosophical problem of some difficulty here, which I do not propose to discuss, but somewhere among all the possible combinations of letters that can occur are what one may call the *real* names of God. By systematic permutation of letters, we have been trying to list them all.'

'I see. You've been starting at AAAAAAA . . . and working up to ZZZZZZZ . . .'

'Exactly – though we use a special alphabet of our own. Modifying the electromatic typewriters to deal with this is, of course, trivial. A rather more interesting problem is that of devising suitable circuits to eliminate ridiculous combinations. For example, no letter must occur more than three times in succession.'

'Three? Surely you mean two.'

'Three is correct: I am afraid it would take too long to explain why, even if you understood our language.'

'I'm sure it would,' said Wagner hastily. 'Go on.'

'Luckily, it will be a simple matter to adapt your Automatic Sequence Computer for this work, since once it has been programmed properly it will permute each letter in turn and print the result. What would have taken us fifteen thousand years it will be able to do in a hundred days.'

Dr Wagner was scarcely conscious of the faint sounds from the Manhattan streets far below. He was in a different world, a world of natural, not man-made, mountains. High up in their remote aeries these monks had been patiently at work, generation after generation, compiling their lists of meaningless words. Was there any limit to the follies of mankind? Still, he must give no hint of his inner thoughts. The customer was always right . . .

'There's no doubt,' replied the doctor, 'that we can modify the Mark V to print lists of this nature. I'm much more worried about the problem of installation and maintenance. Getting out to Tibet, in these days, is not going to be easy.'

'We can arrange that. The components are small enough to travel by air – that is one reason why we chose your machine. If you can get them to India, we will provide transport from there.'

'And you want to hire two of our engineers?'

'Yes, for the three months that the project should occupy.'

'I've no doubt that Personnel can manage that.' Dr Wagner scribbled a note on his desk pad. 'There are just two other points –'

Before he could finish the sentence the lama had produced a small slip of paper.

'This is my certified credit balance at the Asiatic Bank.'

'Thank you. It appears to be – ah – adequate. The second matter is so trivial that I hesitate to mention it – but it's surprising how often the obvious gets overlooked. What source of electrical energy have you?'

'A diesel generator providing fifty kilowatts at a hundred and ten volts. It was installed about five years ago and is quite reliable. It's made life at the lamasery much more comfortable, but of course it was really installed to provide power for the motors driving the prayer wheels.'

'Of course,' echoed Dr Wagner. 'I should have thought of that.'

The view from the parapet was vertiginous, but in time one gets used to anything. After three months, George Hanley was not impressed by the two-thousand-foot swoop into the abyss or the remote checkerboard of fields in the valley below. He was leaning against the wind-smoothed stones and staring morosely at the distant mountains whose names he had never bothered to discover.

This, thought George, was the craziest thing that had ever happened to him. 'Project Shangri-La', some wit back at the labs had christened it. For weeks now the Mark V had been churning out acres of sheets covered with gibberish. Patiently, inexorably, the computer had been rearranging letters in all their possible combinations, exhausting each class before going on to the next. As the sheets had emerged from the electromatic typewriters, the monks had carefully cut them up and pasted them into enormous books. In another week, heaven be praised, they would have finished. Just what obscure calculations had convinced the monks that they needn't bother to go on to words of ten, twenty, or a hundred letters, George didn't know. One of his recurring nightmares was that there would be some change of plan, and that the high lama (whom they'd naturally called Sam Jaffe, though he didn't look a bit like him) would suddenly announce that the project would be extended to approximately AD 2060. They were quite capable of it.

George heard the heavy wooden door slam in the wind as Chuck came out on to the parapet beside him. As usual, Chuck was smoking one of the cigars that made him so popular with the monks – who, it seemed, were quite willing to embrace all the minor and most of the major pleasures of life. That was one thing in their favour: they might be crazy, but they weren't bluenoses. Those frequent trips they took down to the village, for instance . . .

'Listen, George,' said Chuck urgently. 'I've learned something that means trouble.'

'What's wrong? Isn't the machine behaving?' That was the worst contingency George could imagine. It might delay his return, and no thing could be more horrible. The way he felt now, even the sight of a TV commercial would seem like manna from heaven. At least it would be some link with home.

'No – it's nothing like that.' Chuck settled himself on the parapet, which was unusual because normally he was scared of the drop. 'I've just found what all this is about.'

'What d'ya mean? I thought we knew.'

'Sure – we know what the monks are trying to do. But we didn't know why. It's the craziest thing –'

'Tell me something new,' growled George.

'– but old Sam's just come clean with me. You know the way he drops in every afternoon to watch the sheets roll out. Well, this time he seemed rather excited, or at least as near as he'll ever get to it. When I told him that we were on the last cycle he asked me, in that cute English accent of his, if I'd ever wondered what they were trying to do. I said, "Sure" – and he told me.'

'Go on: I'll buy it.'

'Well, they believe that when they have listed all His names – and they reckon that there are about nine billion of them – God's purpose will be achieved. The human race will have finished what it was created to do, and there won't be any point in carrying on. Indeed, the very idea is something like blasphemy.'

'Then what do they expect us to do? Commit suicide?'

'There's no need for that. When the list's completed, God steps in and simply winds things up . . . bingo!'

'Oh, I get it. When we finish our job, it will be the end of the world.'

Chuck gave a nervous little laugh.

'That's just what I said to Sam. And do you know what happened? He looked at me in a very queer way, like I'd been stupid in class, and said, "It's nothing as trivial as *that*."'

George thought this over for a moment.

'That's what I call taking the Wide View,' he said presently. 'But what d'you suppose we should do about it? I don't see that it makes the slightest difference to us. After all, we already knew that they were crazy.'

'Yes — but don't you see what may happen? When the list's complete and the Last Trump doesn't blow — or whatever it is they expect — *we* may get the blame. It's our machine they've been using. I don't like the situation one little bit.'

'I see,' said George slowly. 'You've a point there. But this sort of thing's happened before, you know. When I was a kid down in Louisiana we had a crackpot preacher who once said the world was going to end next Sunday. Hundreds of people believed him — even sold their homes. Yet when nothing happened, they didn't turn nasty, as you'd expect. They just decided that he'd made a mistake in his calculations and went right on believing. I guess some of them still do.'

'Well, this isn't Louisiana, in case you hadn't noticed. There are just two of us and hundreds of these monks. I like them, and I'll be sorry for old Sam when his life backfires on him. But all the same, I wish I was somewhere else.'

'I've been wishing that for weeks. But there's nothing we can do until the contract's finished and the transport arrives to fly us out.'

'Of course,' said Chuck thoughtfully, 'we could always try a bit of sabotage.'

'Like hell we could! That would make things worse.'

'Not the way I meant. Look at it like this. The machine will finish its run four days from now, on the present twenty-hours-a-day basis. The transport calls in a week. OK – then all we need to do is to find something that needs replacing during one of the overhaul periods – something that will hold up the works for a couple of days. We'll fix it, of course, but not too quickly. If we time matters properly, we can be down at the airfield when the last name pops out of the register. They won't be able to catch us then.'

'I don't like it,' said George. 'It will be the first time I ever walked out on a job. Besides, it would make them suspicious. No, I'll sit tight and take what comes.'

'I *still* don't like it,' he said, seven days later, as the tough little mountain ponies carried them down the winding road. 'And don't you think I'm running away because I'm afraid. I'm just sorry for those poor old guys up there, and I don't want to be around when they find what suckers they've been. Wonder how Sam will take it?'

'It's funny,' replied Chuck, 'but when I said goodbye I got the idea he knew we were walking out on him – and that he didn't care because he knew the machine was running smoothly and that the job would soon be finished. After that – well, of course, for him there just isn't any After That . . .'

George turned in his saddle and stared back up the mountain road. This was the last place from which one could get a clear view of the lamasery. The squat, angular buildings were silhouetted against the after-glow of the sunset: here and there, lights gleamed like portholes in the side of an ocean liner. Electric lights, of course, sharing the same circuit as the Mark V. How much longer would they share it? wondered George. Would the monks smash up the computer in their rage and disappointment? Or would they just sit down quietly and begin their calculations all over again?

He knew exactly what was happening up on the mountain at this very moment. The high lama and his assistants would be sitting in their silk robes, inspecting the sheets as the junior monks carried them away from the typewriters and pasted them into the great volumes. No one would be saying anything. The only sound would be the incessant patter, the never-ending rainstorm of the keys hitting the paper, for the Mark V itself was utterly silent as it flashed through its thousands of calculations a second. Three months of this, thought George, was enough to start anyone climbing up the wall.

'There she is!' called Chuck, pointing down into the valley. 'Ain't she beautiful!'

She certainly was, thought George. The battered old DC3 lay at the end of the runway like a tiny silver cross. In two hours she would be bearing then away to freedom and sanity. It was a thought worth savouring like a fine liqueur. George let it roll round his mind as the pony trudged patiently down the slope.

The swift night of the high Himalayas was now almost upon them. Fortunately, the road was very good, as roads went in that region, and they were both carrying torches. There was not the slightest danger, only a certain discomfort from the bitter cold. The sky overhead was perfectly clear, and ablaze with the familiar, friendly stars. At least there would be no risk, thought George, of the pilot being unable to take off because of weather conditions. That had been his only remaining worry.

He began to sing, but gave it up after a while. This vast arena of mountains, gleaming like whitely hooded ghosts on every side, did not encourage such ebullience. Presently George glanced at his watch.

'Should be there in an hour,' he called back over his shoulder to Chuck. Then he added, in an afterthought: 'Wonder if the computer's finished its run. It was due about now.'

Chuck didn't reply, so George swung round in his saddle. He could just see Chuck's face, a white oval turned towards the sky.

'Look,' whispered Chuck, and George lifted his eyes to heaven. (There is always a last time for everything.)

Overhead, without any fuss, the stars were going out.

There Will Come Soft Rains

RAY BRADBURY

If Ray Bradbury were to be dissected, the following elements would be found to be present: poet, workaholic, mystic, spellbinder, folklorist, craftsman and firework manufacturer. The last is important. His prose crackles, sparkles, glitters, explodes.

He has produced countless long and short stories over the last half-century. They are easily found – his work is printed and reprinted in his home country (USA) and all over the world.

In the living room the voice-clock sang, *Tick-tock, seven o'clock, time to get up, time to get up, seven o'clock!* as if it were afraid that nobody would. The morning house lay empty. The clock ticked on, repeating its sounds into the emptiness. *Seven-nine, breakfast time, seven-nine!*

In the kitchen the breakfast stove gave a hissing sigh and ejected from its warm interiors eight pieces of perfectly browned toast, eight eggs sunny-side up, sixteen slices of bacon, two coffees, and two cool glasses of milk.

'Today is August 4, 2026,' said a second voice from the kitchen ceiling, 'in the city of Allendale, California.' It repeated the date three times for memory's sake. 'Today is Mr Featherstone's birthday. Today is the anniversary of Tilita's marriage. Insurance is payable, as are the water, gas, and light bills.'

Somewhere in the walls, relays clicked, memory tapes glided under electric eyes.

Eight-one, tick-tock, eight-one o'clock, off to school, off to work, run, run, eight-one! but no doors slammed, no carpets took the soft tread of rubber heels. It was raining outside. The weather box on the front door sang quietly: 'Rain, rain, go away; boots and raincoats for today . . .' And the rain tapped on the empty house, echoing.

Outside, the garage chimed and lifted its door to reveal the waiting car. After a long wait the door swung down again.

At eight-thirty the eggs were shrivelled and the toast was like stone. An aluminium wedge scraped them into the sink, where hot water whirled them down a metal throat which digested and flushed them away to the distant sea. The dirty dishes were dropped into a hot washer and emerged twinkling dry.

Nine-fifteen, sang the clock, *time to clean.*

Out of warrens in the wall, tiny robot mice darted. The rooms were a-crawl with the small cleaning animals, all rubber and metal. They thudded against chairs, whirling their moustached runners, kneading the rug nap, sucking gently at hidden dust. Then, like mysterious invaders, they popped into their burrows. Their pink electric eyes faded. The house was clean.

Ten o'clock. The sun came out from behind the rain. The house stood alone in a city of rubble and ashes. This was the one house left standing. At night the ruined city gave off a radioactive glow which could be seen for miles.

Ten-fifteen. The garden sprinklers whirled up in golden founts, filling the soft morning air with scatterings of brightness. The water pelted window-panes, running down the charred west side where the house had been burned evenly free of its white paint. The entire west face of the house was black, save for five places. Here the silhouette in paint of a man mowing a lawn. Here, as in a photograph, a woman bent to pick flowers. Still farther over, their images burnt on wood in one titanic instant, a small boy, hands flung into the air; higher up, the image of a thrown ball, and opposite him a girl, hands raised to catch a ball which never came down.

The five spots of paint – the man, the woman, the children, the ball – remained. The rest was a thin charcoaled layer.

The gentle sprinkler rain filled the garden with falling light.

Until this day, how well the house had kept its peace! How carefully it had inquired, 'Who goes there? What's the password?' and, getting no answer from lonely foxes and whining cats, it had shut up its windows and drawn shades in an old-maidenly preoccupation with self-protection which bordered on a mechanical paranoia.

It quivered at each sound, the house did. If a sparrow brushed a window, the shade snapped up. The bird, startled, flew off! No, not even a bird must touch the house!

The house was an altar with ten thousand attendants, big, small, servicing, attending, in choirs. But the gods had gone away, and the ritual of the religion continued senselessly, uselessly.

Twelve noon.

A dog whined, shivering, on the front porch.

The front door recognized the dog voice and opened. The dog, once huge and fleshy, but now gone to bone and covered with sores, moved in and through the house, tracking mud. Behind it whirred angry mice, angry at having to pick up mud, angry at inconvenience.

For not a leaf fragment blew under the door but what the wall-panels flipped open and the copper scrap rats flashed swiftly out. The offending dust, hair, or paper, seized in miniature steel jaws, was raced back to the burrows. There, down tubes which fed into the cellar, it was dropped into the sighing vent of an incinerator which sat like evil Baal in a dark corner.

The dog ran upstairs, hysterically yelping to each door, at last realizing, as the house realized, that only silence was here.

It sniffed the air and scratched the kitchen door. Behind the door, the stove was making pancakes which filled the house with a rich baked odour and the scent of maple syrup.

The dog frothed at the mouth, lying at the door, sniffing, its eyes turned to fire. It ran wildly in circles, biting at its tail, spun in a frenzy, and died. It lay in the parlour for an hour.

Two o'clock, sang a voice.

Delicately sensing decay at last, the regiments of mice hummed out as softly as blown grey leaves in an electrical wind.

Two-fifteen.

The dog was gone.

In the cellar, the incinerator glowed suddenly and a whirl of sparks leaped up the chimney.

Two thirty-five.

Bridge tables sprouted from patio walls. Playing-cards fluttered on to pads in a shower of pips. Martinis manifested on an oaken bench with egg-salad sandwiches. Music played.

But the tables were silent and the cards untouched.

At four o'clock the tables folded like great butterflies back through the panelled walls.

Four-thirty.

The nursery walls glowed.

Animals took shape: yellow giraffes, blue lions, pink antelopes, lilac panthers cavorting in crystal substance. The walls were glass. They looked out upon colour and fantasy. Hidden films clocked through well-oiled sprockets, and the walls lived. The nursery floor was woven to resemble a crisp, cereal meadow. Over this ran aluminium roaches and iron crickets, and in the hot, still air butterflies of delicate red tissue wavered among the sharp aroma of animal spoors! There was the sound like a great matted yellow hive of bees within a dark bellows, the lazy bumble of a purring lion. And there was the patter of okapi feet and the murmur of a fresh jungle rain, like other hoofs, falling upon the summer-starched grass. Now the walls dissolved into distances of parched weed, mile on mile, and warm, endless sky. The animals drew away into thornbrakes and water-holes.

It was the children's hour.

Five o'clock. The bath filled with clear hot water.

Six, seven, eight o'clock. The dinner dishes manipulated like magic tricks, and in the study a *click.* In the metal stand opposite the hearth where a fire now blazed up warmly, a cigar popped out, half an inch of soft grey ash on it, smoking, waiting.

Nine o'clock. The beds warmed their hidden circuits, for nights were cool here.

Nine-five. A voice spoke from the study ceiling:

'Mrs McClellan, which poem would you like this evening?'

The house was silent.

The voice said at last, 'Since you express no preference, I shall select a poem at random.' Quiet music rose to back the voice. 'Sara Teasdale. As I recall, your favourite . . .

There will come soft rains and the smell of the ground,
The swallows circling with their shimmering sound;

And frogs in the pools singing at night,
And wild plum-trees in tremulous white;

Robins will wear their feathery fire,
Whistling their whims on a low fence-wire;

And not one will know of the war, not one
Will care at last when it is done.

Not one would mind, neither bird nor tree,
If mankind perished utterly;

And Spring herself, when she woke at dawn,
Would scarcely know that we were gone.'

The fire burned on the stone hearth and the cigar fell away into a mound of quiet ash on its tray. The empty chairs faced each other between the silent walls, and the music played.

At ten o'clock the house began to die.
The wind blew. A falling tree-bough crashed through

the kitchen window. Cleaning solvent, bottled, shat-tered over the stove. The room was ablaze in an instant!

'Fire!' screamed a voice. The house-lights flashed, water-pumps shot water from the ceilings. But the solvent spread on the linoleum, licking, eating, under the kitchen door, while the voices took it up in chorus: 'Fire, fire, fire!'

The house tried to save itself. Doors sprang tightly shut, but the windows were broken by the heat, and the wind blew and sucked upon the fire.

The house gave ground as the fire in ten billion angry sparks moved with flaming ease from room to room and then up the stairs. While scurrying water-rats squeaked from the walls, pistolled their water, and ran for more. And the wall-sprays let down showers of mechanical rain.

But too late. Somewhere, sighing, a pump shrugged to a stop. The quenching rain ceased. The reserve water supply which had filled baths and washed dishes for many quiet days was gone.

The fire crackled up the stairs. It fed upon Picassos and Matisses in the upper halls, like delicacies, baking off the oily flesh, tenderly crisping the canvases into black shavings.

Now the fire lay in beds, stood in windows, changed the colours of drapes!

And then, reinforcements.

From attic trapdoors, blind robot faces peered down with faucet mouths gushing green chemical.

The fire backed off, as even an elephant must at the

sight of a dead snake. Now there were twenty snakes whipping over the floor, killing the fire with a clear, cold venom of green froth.

But the fire was clever. It had sent flame outside the house, up through the attic to the pumps there. An explosion! The attic brain which directed the pumps was shattered into bronze shrapnel on the beams.

The fire rushed back into every closet and felt the clothes hung there.

The house shuddered, oak bone on bone, its bared skeleton cringing from the heat, its wire, its nerves revealed as if a surgeon had torn the skin off to let the red veins and capillaries quiver in the scalded air. Help, help! Fire! Run, run! Heat snapped mirrors like the first brittle winter ice. And the voices wailed Fire, fire, run, run, like a tragic nursery rhyme, a dozen voices, high, low, like children dying in a forest, alone, alone. And the voices fading as the wires popped their sheathings like hot chestnuts. One, two, three, four, five voices died.

In the nursery the jungle burned. Blue lions roared, purple giraffes bounded off. The panthers ran in circles, changing colour, and ten million animals, running before the fire, vanished off towards a distant steaming river . . .

Ten more voices died. In the last instant under the fire avalanche, other choruses, oblivious, could be heard announcing the time, playing music, cutting the lawn by remote-control mower, or setting an umbrella frantically out and in the slamming and opening front door, a thousand things happening, like a clock-shop when each clock strikes the hour insanely before or after the other, a scene of maniac confusion, yet unity; singing, screaming, a few last cleaning mice darting bravely out to carry the horrid ashes away! And one voice, with sublime disregard for the situation, read poetry aloud in the fiery study, until all the film-spools burned, until all the wires withered and the circuits cracked.

The fire burst the house and let it slam flat down, puffing out skirts of spark and smoke.

In the kitchen, an instant before the rain of fire and timber, the stove could be seen making breakfasts at a psychopathic rate, ten dozen eggs, six loaves of toast, twenty dozen bacon strips, which, eaten by fire, started the stove working again, hysterically hissing!

The crash. The attic smashing into kitchen and parlour. The parlour into cellar, cellar into sub-cellar. Deep freeze, armchair, film tapes, circuits, beds, and all like skeletons thrown in a cluttered mound deep under.

Smoke and silence. A great quantity of smoke.

Dawn showed faintly in the east. Among the ruins, one wall stood alone. Within the wall, a last voice said, over and over again and again, even as the sun rose to shine upon the heaped rubble and steam:

'Today is August 5, 2026, today is August 5, 2026, today is . . .'

Flowers for Algernon

DANIEL KEYES

It is not often that a SF tale may be described as 'touching', 'sadly beautiful' or 'lastingly memorable'. This one can be. It lingers in the mind. Its American author, unlike most other science fiction 'greats', seems to have produced little else in the genre. But this one story is enough. Of course it collected awards and distinctions in its time: and may well find a place in our century's list of 'Finest Short Stories'.

progris riport 1 – martch 5 1965
DR STRAUSS SAYS I SHUD RITE DOWN what I think and evrey thing that happins to me from now on. I dont know why but he says its important so they will see if they will use me. I hope they use me. Miss Kinnian says maybe they can make me smart. I want to be smart. My name is Charlie Gordon. I

am 37 years old and 2 weeks ago was my birthday. I have nuthing more to rite now so I will close for today.

progris riport 2 – martch 6

I had a test today. I think I faled it. and I think that maybe now they wont use me. What happind is a nice young man was in the room and he had some white cards with ink spilled all over them. He sed Charlie what do you see on this card. I was very skared even tho I had my rabits foot in my pockit because when I was a kid I always faled tests in school and I spilled ink to.

I told him I saw a inkblot. He said yes and it made me feel good. I thot that was all but when I got up to go he stopped me. He said now sit down Charlie we are not thru yet. Then I dont remember so good but he wantid me to say what was in the ink. I dint see nuthing in the ink but he said there was picturs there other pepul saw some picturs. I coudnt see any picturs. I reely tryed to see. I held the card close up and then far away. Then I said if I had my glases I coud see better I usally only ware my glases in the movies or TV but I said they are in the closit in the hall. I got them. Then I said let me see that card agen I bet Ill find it now.

I tryed hard but I still coudnt find the picturs I only saw the ink. I told him maybe I need new glases. He rote somthing down on a paper and I got skared of faling the test. I told him it was a very nice inkblot with littel points all around the eges. He looked very sad so that wasnt it. I said please let me try agen. Ill get it in a few minits becaus Im not so fast somtimes. Im a slow reeder too in Miss Kinnians class for slow adults but I'm trying very hard.

He gave me a chance with another card that had 2 kinds of ink spilled on it red and blue.

He was very nice and talked slow like Miss Kinnian does and he explaned it to me that it was a *raw shok*. He said pepul see things in the ink. I said show me where. He said think. I told him I think a inkblot but that wasnt rite eather. He said what does it remind you – pretend something. I closd my eyes for a long time to pretend. I told him I pretned a fowntan pen with ink leeking all over a table cloth. Then he got up and went out.

I dont think I passd the *raw shok* test.

progris report 3 – martch 7

Dr Strauss and Dr Nemur say it dont matter about the inkblots. I told them I dint spill the ink on the cards and I coudnt see anything in the ink. They said that maybe they will still use me. I said Miss Kinnian never gave me tests like that one only spelling and reading. They said Miss Kinnian told that I was her bestist pupil in the adult nite scool becaus I tryed the hardist and I reely wantid to lern. They said how come you went to the adult nite scool all by yourself Charlie. How did you find it. I said I askd pepul and sumbody told me where I shud go to lern to read and spell good. They said why did you want to. I told them becaus all my life I wantid to be smart and not dumb. But its very hard to be smart. They said you know it will probly be tempirery. I said yes. Miss Kinnian told me. I dont care if it herts.

Later I had more crazy tests today. The nice lady who gave it me told me the name and I asked her how do you spellit so I can rite it in my progris riport. THEMATIC APPERCEPTION TEST. I dont know the frist 2 words but I know what *test* means. You got to pass it or you get bad marks. This test lookd easy becaus I coud see the picturs. Only this time she dint want me to tell her the picturs. That mixd me up. I said the man yesterday said I shoud tell him what I saw in the ink she said that dont make no difrence. She said make up storys about the pepul in the picturs.

I told her how can you tell storys about pepul you never met. I said why shud I make up lies. I never tell lies any more becaus I always get caut.

She told me this test and the other one the raw-shok was for getting personalty. I laffed so hard. I said how can you get that thing from inkblots and fotos. She got sore and put her picturs away. I dont care. It was sily. I gess I faled that test too.

Later some men in white coats took me to a difernt part of the hospitil and gave me a game to play. It was like a race with a white mouse. They called the mouse Algernon. Algernon was in a box with a lot of twists and turns like all kinds of walls and they gave me a pencil and a paper with lines and lots of boxes.

On one side is said START and on the other end it said FINISH. They said it was *amazed* and that Algernon and me had the same *amazed* to do. I dint see how we could have the same *amazed* if Algernon had a box and I had a paper but I dint say nothing. Anyway there wasnt time because the race started.

One of the men had a watch he was trying to hide so I woudnt see it so I tryed not to look and that made me nervus.

Anyway that test made me feel worser than all the others because they did it over 10 times with difernt *amazeds* and Algernon won every time. I dint know that mice were so smart. Maybe thats because Algernon is a white mouse. Maybe white mice are smarter then other mice.

progris riport 4 — Mar 8

Their going to use me! Im so exited I can hardly write. Dr Nemur and Dr Strauss had a argament about it first. Dr Nemur was in the office when Dr Strauss brot me in. Dr Nemur was worryed about using me but Dr Strauss told him Miss Kinnian rekemmended me the best from all the people who she was teaching. I like Miss Kinnian becaus shes a very smart teacher. And she said Charlie your going to have a second chance. If you volenteer for this experament you mite get smart. They dont know if it will be perminint but theirs a chance. Thats why I said ok even when I was scared because she said it was an operashun. She said dont be scared Charlie you done so much with so little I think you deserv it most of all.

So I got scaird when Dr Nemur and Dr Strauss argud about it. Dr Strauss said I had something that was very good. He said I had a good *motor-vation*. I never even knew I had that. I felt proud when he said that not everybody with an eye-q of 68 had that thing. I dont know what it is or where I got it but he said Algernon had it too. Algernons *motor-vation* is the cheese they put in his box. But it cant be that because I didnt eat any cheese this week.

Then he told Dr Nemur something I dint understand so while they were talking I wrote down some of the words.

He said Dr Nemur I know Charlie is not what you had in mind as the first of your new brede of intelek★ ★ (coudnt get the word) superman. But most people of his low ment★★ are host★★ and uncoop★★ they are usualy dull apath★★ and hard to reach. He has a good natcher hes intristed and eager to please.

Dr Nemur said remember he will be the first human beeng ever to have his intelijence trippled by surgicle meens.

Dr Strauss said exakly. Look at how well hes lerned to read and write for his low mentel age its as grate an acheve★★ as you and I lerning einstines therey of ★★ vity without help. That shows the intenss motor-vation. Its comparat★★ a tremen★★ achev★★ I say we use Charlie.

I dint get all the words and they were talking to

fast but it sounded like Dr Strauss was on my side and like the other one wasnt.

Then Dr Nemur nodded he said all right maybe your right. We will use Charlie. When he said that I got so exited I jumped up and shook his hand for being so good to me. I told him thank you doc you wont be sorry for giving me a second chance. And I mean it like I told him. After the operashun Im gonna try to be smart. Im gonna try awful hard.

progris ript 5 – Mar 10

Im skared. Lots of people who work here and the nurses and the people who gave me the tests came to bring me candy and wish me luck. I hope I have luck. I got my rabits foot and my lucky penny and my horse shoe. Only a black cat crossed me when I was comming to the hospitil. Dr Strauss says dont be supersitis Charlie this is sience. Anyway Im keeping my rabits foot with me.

I asked Dr Strauss if Ill beat Algernon in the race after the operashun and he said maybe. If the operashun works Ill show that mouse I can be as smart as he is. Maybe smarter. Then Ill be abel to read better and spell the words good and know lots of things and be like other people. I want to be smart like other people. If it works perminint they will make everybody smart all over the wurld.

They dint give me anything to eat this morning. I dont know what that eating has to do with getting smart. Im very hungry and Dr Nemur took away my box of candy. That Dr Nemur is a grouch. Dr Strauss says I can have it back after the operashun. You cant eat befor a operashun . . .

Progress Report 6 — Mar 15

The operashun dint hurt. He did it while I was sleeping. They took off the bandijis from my eyes and my head today so I can make a PROGRESS REPORT. Dr Nemur who looked at some of my other ones says I spell PROGRESS wrong and he told me how to spell it and REPORT too. I got to try and remember that.

I have a very bad memary for spelling. Dr Strauss says its ok to tell about all the things that happin to me but he says I shoud tell more about what I feel and what I think. When I told him I dont know how to think he said try. All the time when the bandijis were on my eyes I tryed to think. Nothing happened. I dont know what to think about. Maybe if I ask him he will tell me how I can think now that Im suppose to get smart. What do smart people think about. Fancy things I suppose. I wish I knew some fancy things alredy.

Progress Report 7 — mar 19

Nothing is happining. I had lots of tests and different kinds of races with Algernon. I hate that mouse. He always beats me. Dr Strauss said I got to play those games. And he said some time I got to take those tests over again. The inkblots are stupid. And those pictures are stupid too. I like to draw a picture of a man and a woman but I wont make up lies about people.

I got a headache from trying to think so much. I thot Dr Strauss was my frend but he dont help me. He dont tell me what to think or when Ill get smart. Miss Kinnian dint come to see me. I think writing these progress reports are stupid too.

Progress Report 8 – Mar 23
Im going back to work at the factery. They said it was better I shud go back to work but I cant tell anyone what the operashun was for and I have to come to the hospitil for an hour evry night after work. They are gonna pay me mony every month for lerning to be smart.

Im glad Im going back to work because I miss my job and all my frends and all the fun we have there.

Dr Strauss says I shud keep writing things down but I dont have to do it every day just when I think of something or something speshul happins. He says dont get discoridged because it takes time and it happins slow. He says it took a long time with Algernon before he got 3 times smarter then he was before. Thats why Algernon beats me all the time because he had that operashun too. That makes me feel better. I coud probly do that *amazed* faster than a reglar mouse. Maybe some day Ill beat Algernon. Boy that would be something. So far Algernon looks like he mite be smart perminent.

★

Mar 25 (I dont have to write PROGRESS REPORT on top any more just when I hand it in once a week for Dr Nemur to read. I just have to put the date on. That saves time)

We had a lot of fun at the factery today. Joe Carp said hey look where Charlie had his operashun what did they do Charlie put some brains in. I was going to tell him but I remembered Dr Strauss said no. Then Frank Reilly said what did you do Charlie forget your key and open your door the hard way. That made me laff. Their really my friends and they like me.

Sometimes somebody will say hey look at Joe or Frank or George he really pulled a Charlie Gordon. I dont know why they say that but they always laff. This morning Amos Borg who is the 4 man at Donnegans used my name when he shouted at Ernie the office boy. Ernie lost a packige. He said Ernie for godsake what are you trying to be a Charlie Gordon. I dont understand why he said that. I never lost any packiges.

Mar 28 Dr Strauss came to my room tonight to see why I dint come in like I was suppose to. I told him I dont like to race with Algernon any more. He said I dont have to for a while but I shud come in. He had a present for me only it wasnt a present but just for lend. I thot it was a little television but it wasnt. He said I got to turn it on when I go to sleep. I said your kidding why shud I turn it on when Im going to sleep. Who ever herd of a thing like that. But he said if I want to get smart I got to do what he says. I told him I dint think I was going to get smart and he put his hand on my sholder and said Charlie you dont know it yet but your getting smarter all the time. You wont notice for a while. I think he was just being nice to make me feel good because I dont look any smarter.

Oh yes I almost forgot. I asked him when I can go back to the class at Miss Kinnians school. He said I wont go their. He said that soon Miss Kinnian will come to the hospitil to start and teach me speshul. I was mad at her for not comming to see me when I got the operashun but I like her so maybe we will be frends again.

Mar 29 That crazy TV kept me up all night. How can I sleep with something yelling crazy things all night in my ears. And the nutty pictures. Wow. I dont know what it says when Im up so how am I going to know when Im sleeping.

Dr Strauss says its ok. He says my brains are lerning when I sleep and that will help me when Miss Kinnian starts my lessons in the hospitl (only I found out it isnt a hospitil its a labatory). I think its all crazy. If you can get smart when your sleeping why do people go to school. That thing I dont think will work. I use to watch the late show and the late late show on TV all the time and it never made me smart. Maybe you have to sleep while you watch it.

Progress report 9 – April 3

Dr Strauss showed me how to keep the TV turned low so now I can sleep. I dont hear a thing. And I still dont understand what it says. A few times I play it over in the morning to find out what I lerned when I was sleeping and I dont think so. Miss Kinnian says maybe its another langwidge or something. But most times it sounds american. It talks so fast faster then even Miss Gold who was my teacher in 6 grade and I remember she talked so fast I coudnt understand her.

I told Dr Strauss what good is it to get smart in my sleep. I want to be smart when Im awake. He says its the same thing and I have two minds. Theres the *subconscious* and the *conscious* (thats how you spell it). And one dont tell the other one what its doing. They dont even talk to each other. Thats why I dream. And boy have I been having crazy dreams. Wow. Ever since that night TV. The late late late late late show.

I forgot to ask him if it was only me or if everybody had those two minds.

I just looked up the word in the dictionary Dr Strauss gave me. The word is *subconscious. adj. Of the nature of mental operations yet not present in consciousness; as, subconscious conflict of desires.*) Theres more but I still don't know what it means. This isnt a very good dictionary for dumb people like me.

Anyway the headache is from the party. My frends from the factery Joe Carp and Frank Reilly invited me to go with them to Muggsys Saloon for some

117

drinks. I dont like to drink but they said we will have lots of fun. I had a good time.

Joe Carp said I shoud show the girls how I mop out the toilet in the factory and he got me a mop. I showed them and everyone laffed when I told that Mr Donnegan said I was the best janiter he ever had because I like my job and do it good and never come late or miss a day except for my operashun.

I said Miss Kinnian always said Charlie be proud of your job because you do it good.

Everybody laffed and we had a good time and they gave me lots of drinks and Joe said Charlie is a card when hes potted. I dont know what that means but everybody likes me and we have fun. I cant wait to be smart like my best frends Joe Carp and Frank Reilly.

I dont remember how the party was over but I think I went out to buy a newspaper and coffe for Joe and Frank and when I came back there was no one their. I looked for them all over till late. Then I dont remember so good but I think I got sleepy or sick. A nice cop brot me back home. Thats what my landlady Mrs Flynn says.

But I got a headache and a big lump on my head and black and blue all over. I think maybe I fell but Joe Carp says it was the cop they beat up drunks some times. I don't think so. Miss Kinnian says cops are to help people. Anyway I got a bad headache and Im sick and hurt all over. I dent think Ill drink anymore.

April 6 I beat Algernon! I dint even know I beat him

until Burt the tester told me. Then the second time I lost because I got so exited I fell off the chair before I finished. But after that I beat him 8 more times. I must be getting smart to beat a smart mouse like Algernon. But I don't feel smarter.

I wanted to race Algernon some more but Burt said thats enough for one day. They let me hold him for a minit. Hes not so bad. Hes soft like a ball of cotton. He blinks and when he opens his eyes they black and pink on the eges.

I said can I feed him because I felt bad to beat him and I wanted to be nice and make frends. Burt said no Algernon is a very specshul mouse with an operashun like mine, and he was the first of all the animals to stay smart so long. He told me Algernon is so smart that every day he has to solve a test to get his food. Its a thing like a lock on a door that changes every time Algernon goes in to eat so he has to lern something new to get his food. That made me sad because if he coudnt lern he woud be hungry.

I dont think its right to make you pass a test to eat. How woud Dr Nemur like it to have to pass a test every time he wants to eat. I think Ill be frends with Algernon.

April 9 Tonight after work Miss Kinnian was at the laboratory. She looked like she was glad to see me but scared. I told her dont worry Miss Kinnian Im not smart yet and she laffed. She said I have confidence in you Charlie the way you struggled so hard to read and right better than all the others. At werst you will have it for a littel wile and your doing somthing for sience.

We are reading a very hard book. I never read such a hard book before. Its called *Robinson Crusoe* about a man who gets merooned on a dessert Iland. Hes smart and figers out all kinds of things so he can have a house and food and hes a good swimmer. Only I feel sorry because hes all alone and has no frends. But I think their must be somebody else on the iland because theres a picture with his funny umbrella looking at footprints. I hope he gets a frend and not be lonly.

April 10 Miss Kinnian teaches me to spell better. She says look at a word and close your eyes and say it over and over until you remember. I have lots of truble with *through* that you say *threw* and *enough* and *tough* that you dont say *enew* and *tew*. You got to say *enuff* and *tuff*. Thats how I use to write it before I started to get smart. Im confused but Miss Kinnian says theres no reason in spelling.

Apr 14 Finished *Robinson Crusoe*. I want to find out more about what happens to him but Miss Kinnian says thats all there is. *Why*

Apr 15 Miss Kinnian says Im lerning fast. She read some of the Progress Reports and she looked at me kind of funny. She says Im a fine person and Ill show them all. I asked her why. She said never mind but I shoudnt feel bad if I find out that everybody isnt nice like I think. She said for a person who god gave so little to you done more then a lot of people with brains they never even used. I said all my frends are smart people but there good. They like me and they never did anything that wasnt nice. Then she got something in her eye and she had to run out to the ladys room.

Apr 16 Today, I lerned, the *comma*, this is a comma (,) a period, with a tail, Miss Kinnian, says its importent, because, it makes writing, better, she said, sombeody, coud lose, a lot of money, if a comma, isnt, in the, right place, I dont have, any money, and I dont see, how a comma, keeps you, from losing it,

But she says, everybody, uses commas, so Ill use, them too,

Apr 17 I used the comma wrong. Its punctuation. Miss Kinnian told me to look up long words in the dictionary to lern to spell them. I said whats the difference if you can read it anyway. She said its part of your education so now on Ill look up all the words Im not sure how to spell. It takes a long time to write that way but I think Im remembering. I only have to look up once and after that I get it right. Anyway thats how come I got the word *punctuation* right. (Its that way in the dictionary). Miss Kinnian says a period is punctuation too, and there are lots of other marks to lern. I told her I thot all the periods had to have tails but she said no.

You got to mix them up, she showed? me" how. to mix! them(up,. and now; I can! mix up all kinds" of punctuation, in! my writing? There, are lots! of rules? to lern; but Im gettin'g them in my head.

One thing I? like about, Dear Miss Kinnian: (thats the way it goes in a business letter if I ever go into business) is she, always gives me' a reason" when – I ask. She's a gen'ius! I wish! I cou'd be smart" like, her;

(Punctuation, is; fun!)

April 18 What a dope I am! I didn't even understand what she was talking about. I read the grammar book last night and it explanes the whole thing. Then I saw it was the same way as Miss Kinnian was trying to tell me, but I didn't get it. I got up in the middle of the night, and the whole thing straightened out in my mind.

Miss Kinnian said that the TV working in my sleep helped out. She said I reached a plateau. Thats like the flat top of a hill.

After I figgered out how punctuation worked, I read over all my old Progress Reports from the beginning. Boy, did I have crazy spelling and punctuation! I told Miss Kinnian I ought to go over the pages and fix the mistakes but she said, 'No, Charlie, Dr Nemur wants them just as they are. That's why he let you keep them after they were photostated, to see your own progress. You're coming along fast, Charlie.'

That made me feel good. After the lesson I went down and played with Algernon. We don't race any more.

★

April 20 I feel sick inside. Not sick like for a doctor, but inside my chest it feels empty like getting punched and a heartburn at the same time.

I wasn't going to write about it, but I guess I got to, because it's important. Today was the first time I ever stayed home from work.

Last night Joe Carp and Frank Reilly invited me to a party. There were lots of girls and some men from the factory. I remembered how sick I got last time I drank too much, so I told Joe I didn't want anything to drink. He gave me a plain Coke instead. It tasted funny, but I thought it was just a bad taste in my mouth.

We had a lot of fun for a while. Joe said I should dance with Ellen and she would teach me the steps. I fell a few times and I couldn't understand why because no one else was dancing besides Ellen and me. And all the time I was tripping because somebody's foot was always sticking out.

Then when I got up I saw the look on Joe's face and it gave me a funny feeling in my stomack. 'He's a scream,' one of the girls said. Everybody was laughing.

Frank said, 'I ain't laughed so much since we sent him off for the newspaper that night at Muggsy's and ditched him.'

'Look at him. His face is red.'

'He's blushing. Charlie is blushing.'

'Hey, Ellen, what'd you do to Charlie? I never saw him act like that before.'

I didn't know what to do or where to turn. Everyone was looking at me and laughing and I felt naked. I wanted to hide myself I ran out into the street and I threw up. Then I walked home. It's a funny thing I never knew that Joe and Frank and the others liked to have me around all the time to make fun of me.

Now I know what it means when they say 'to pull a Charlie Gordon.'

I'm ashamed.

Progress report 11

April 21 Still didn't go into the factory. I told Mrs Flynn my landlady to call and tell Mr Donnegan I was sick. Mrs Flynn looks at me very funny lately like she's scared of me.

I think it's a good thing about finding out how everybody laughs at me. I thought about it a lot. It's because I'm so dumb and I don't even know when I'm doing something dumb. People think it's funny when a dumb person can't do things the same way they can.

Anyway, now I know I'm getting smarter every day. I know punctuation and I can spell good. I like to look up all the hard words in the dictionary and remember them. I'm reading a lot now, and Miss Kinnian says I read very fast. Sometimes I even understand what I'm reading about, and it stays in my mind. There are times when I can close my eyes and think of a page and it all comes back like a picture.

Besides history, geography, and arithmetic, Miss

Kinnian said I should start to learn a few foreign languages. Dr Strauss gave me some more tapes to play while I sleep. I still don't understand how that conscious and unconscious mind works, but Dr Strauss says not to worry yet. He asked me to promise that when I start learning college subjects next week I wouldn't read any books on psychology – that is, until he gives me permission.

I feel a lot better today, but I guess I'm still a little angry that all the time people were laughing and making fun of me because I wasn't so smart. When I become intelligent like Dr Strauss says, with three times my I.Q. of 68, then maybe I'll be like everyone else and people will like me and be friendly.

I'm not sure what an I.Q. is. Dr Nemur said it was something that measured how intelligent you were – like a scale in the drugstore weighs pounds. But Dr Strauss had a big argument with him and said an I.Q. didn't weigh intelligence at all. He said an I.Q. showed how much intelligence you could get, like the numbers on the outside of a measuring cup. You still had to fill the cup up with stuff.

Then when I asked Burt, who gives me my intelligence tests and works with Algernon, he said that both of them were wrong (only I had to promise not to tell them he said so). Burt says that the I.Q. measures a lot of different things including some of the things you learned already, and it really isn't any good at all.

So I still don't know what I.Q. is except that mine

is going to be over 200 soon. I didn't want to say anything, but I don't see how if they don't know *what* it is, or *where* it is – I don't see how they know *how much* of it you've got.

Dr Nemur says I have to take a *Rorshach Test* tomorrow. I wonder what *that* is.

April 22 I found out what a *Rorshach* is. It's the test I took before the operation – the one with the inkblots on the pieces of cardboard. The man who gave me the test was the same one.

I was scared to death of those inkblots. I knew he was going to ask me to find the pictures and I knew I wouldn't be able to. I was thinking to myself, if only there was some way of knowing what kind of pictures were hidden there. Maybe there weren't any pictures at all. Maybe it was just a trick to see if I was dumb enough to look for something that wasn't there. Just thinking about that made me sore at him.

'All right, Charlie,' he said, 'you've seen these cards before, remember?'

'Of course I remember.'

The way I said it, he knew I was angry, and he looked surprised. 'Yes, of course. Now I want you to look at this one. What might this be? What do you see on this card? People see all sorts of things in these inkblots. Tell me what it might be for you – what it makes you think of.'

I was shocked. That wasn't what I had expected him to say at all. 'You mean there are no pictures hidden in those inkblots?'

He frowned and took off his glasses. 'What?'

'Pictures. Hidden in the inkblots. Last time you told me that everyone could see them and you wanted me to find them too.'

He explained to me that the last time he had used almost the exact same words he was using now. I didn't believe it, and I still have the suspicion that he misled me at the time just for the fun of it. Unless – I don't know any more – could I have been *that* feeble-minded?

We went through the cards slowly. One of them looked like a pair of bats tugging at something. Another one looked like two men fencing with swords. I imagined all sorts of things. I guess I got carried away. But I didn't trust him any more, and I kept turning them around and even looking on the back to see if there was anything there I was supposed to catch. While he was making his notes, I peeked out of the corner of my eye to read it. But it was all in code that looked like this:

WF + A DdF–Ad orig. WF–A SF + obj

The test still doesn't make sense to me. It seems to me that anyone could make up lies about things that they didn't really see. How could he know I wasn't making a fool of him by mentioning things that I didn't really imagine? Maybe I'll understand it when Dr Strauss lets me read up on psychology.

April 25 I figured out a new way to line up the

machines in the factory, and Mr Donnegan says it will save him ten thousand dollars a year in labour and increased production. He gave me a twenty-five-dollar bonus.

I wanted to take Joe Carp and Frank Reilly out to lunch to celebrate, but Joe said he had to buy some things for his wife, and Frank said he was meeting his cousin for lunch. I guess it'll take a little time for them to get used to the changes in me. Everybody seems to be frightened of me. When I went over to Amos Borg and tapped him on the shoulder, he jumped up in the air.

People don't talk to me much any more or kid around the way they used to. It makes the job kind of lonely.

April 27 I got up the nerve today to ask Miss Kinnian to have dinner with me tomorrow night to celebrate my bonus.

At first she wasn't sure it was right, but I asked Dr Strauss and he said it was OK. Dr Strauss and Dr Nemur don't seem to be getting along so well. They're arguing all the time. This evening when I came in to ask Dr Strauss about having dinner with Miss Kinnian, I heard them shouting. Dr Nemur was saying that it was *his* experiment and *his* research, and Dr Strauss was shouting back that he contributed just as much, because he found me through Miss Kinnian and he performed the operation. Dr Strauss said that someday thousands of neuro-surgeons might be using his technique all over the world.

Dr Nemur wanted to publish the results of the experiment at the end of this month. Dr Strauss wanted to wait a while longer to be sure. Dr Strauss said that Dr Nemur was more interested in the Chair of Psychology at Princeton than he was in the experiment. Dr Nemur said that Dr Strauss was nothing but an opportunist who was trying to ride to glory on *his* coat-tails.

When I left afterwards, I found myself trembling. I don't know why for sure, but it was as if I'd seen both men clearly for the first time. I remember hearing Burt say that Dr Nemur had a shrew of a wife who was pushing him all the time to get things published so that he could become famous. Burt said that the dream of her life was to have a big-shot husband.

Was Dr Strauss really trying to ride on his coat-tails?

April 28 I don't understand why I never noticed how beautiful Miss Kinnian really is. She has brown eyes and feathery brown hair that comes to the top of her neck. She's only thirty-four! I think from the beginning I had the feeling that she was an unreachable genius – and very, very old. Now, every time I see her she grows younger and more lovely.

We had dinner and a long talk. When she said that I was coming along so fast that soon I'd be leaving her behind, I laughed.

'It's true, Charlie. You're already a better reader than I am. You can read a whole page at a glance while I can take in only a few lines at a time. And you remember every single thing you read. I'm lucky if I can recall the main thoughts and the general meaning.'

'I don't feel intelligent. There are so many things I don't understand.'

She took out a cigarette and I lit it for her. 'You've got to be a *little* patient. You're accomplishing in days and weeks what it takes normal people to do in half a lifetime. That's what makes it so amazing. You're like a giant sponge now, soaking things in. Facts, figures, general knowledge. And soon you'll begin to connect them, too. You'll see how the different branches of learning are related. There are many levels, Charlie, like steps on a giant ladder that take you up higher and higher to see more and more of the world around you.

'I can see only a little bit of that, Charlie, and I won't go much higher than I am now, but you'll keep climbing up and up, and see more and more, and each step will open new worlds that you never even knew existed.' She frowned. 'I hope . . . I just hope to God –'

'What?'

'Never mind, Charles. I just hope I wasn't wrong to advise you to go into this in the first place.'

I laughed. 'How could that be? It worked, didn't it? Even Algernon is still smart.'

We sat there silently for a while and I knew what she was thinking about as she watched me toying with the chain of my rabbit's foot and my keys. I didn't want to think of that possibility any more than elderly people want to think of death. I *knew* that this was only the beginning. I knew what she meant about levels because I'd seen some of them already. The thought of leaving her behind made me sad.

I'm in love with Miss Kinnian.

Progress report 12
April 30 I've quit my job with Donnegan's Plastic Box Company. Mr Donnegan insisted that it would be better for all concerned if I left. What did I do to make them hate me so?

The first I knew of it was when Mr Donnegan showed me the petition. Eight hundred and forty names, everyone connected with the factory, except Fanny Girden. Scanning the list quickly, I saw at once that hers was the only missing name. All the rest demanded that I be fired.

Joe Carp and Frank Reilly wouldn't talk to me about it. No one else would either, except Fanny. She was one of the few people I'd known who set her mind to something and believed it no matter what the rest of the world proved, said, or did – and Fanny did not believe that I should have been fired. She had been against the petition on principle and despite the pressure and threats she'd held out.

'Which don't mean to say,' she remarked, 'that I don't think there's something mighty strange about you, Charlie. Them changes. I don't know. You used to be a good, dependable, ordinary man – not too bright maybe, but honest. Who knows what you done to yourself to get so smart all of a sudden. Like everybody around here's been saying, Charlie, it's not right.'

'But how can you say that, Fanny? What's wrong with a man becoming intelligent and wanting to acquire knowledge and understanding of the world around him?'

She stared down at her work and I turned to leave. Without looking at me, she said: 'It was evil when Eve listened to the snake and ate from the tree of knowledge. It was evil when she saw that she was naked. If not for that none of us would ever have to grow old and sick, and die.'

Once again now I have the feeling of shame burning inside me. This intelligence has driven a wedge between me and all the people I once knew and loved. Before, they laughed at me and despised me for my ignorance and dullness; now, they hate me for my knowledge and understanding. What in God's name do they want of me?

They've driven me out of the factory. Now I'm more alone than ever before . . .

May 15 Dr Strauss is very angry at me for not having written any progress reports in two weeks. He's justified because the lab is now paying me a regular salary. I told him I was too busy thinking and reading. When

I pointed out that writing was such a slow process that it made me impatient with my poor handwriting, he suggested that I learn to type. It's much easier to write now because I can type nearly seventy-five words a minute. Dr Strauss continually reminds me of the need to speak and write simply so that people will be able to understand me.

I'll try to review all the things that happened to me during the last two weeks. Algernon and I were presented to the American Psychological Association sitting in convention with the World Psychological Association last Tuesday. We created quite a sensation. Dr Nemur and Dr Strauss were proud of us.

I suspect that Dr Nemur, who is sixty – ten years older than Dr Strauss – finds it necessary to see tangible results of his work. Undoubtedly the result of pressure by Mrs Nemur.

Contrary to my earlier impressions of him, I realize that Dr Nemur is not at all a genius. He has a very good mind, but it struggles under the spectre of self-doubt. He wants people to take him for a genius. Therefore, it is important for him to feel that his work is accepted by the world. I believe that Dr Nemur was afraid of further delay because he worried that someone else might make a discovery along these lines and take the credit from him.

Dr Strauss on the other hand might be called a genius, although I feel that his areas of knowledge are too limited. He was educated in the tradition of narrow specialization; the broader aspects of background

were neglected far more than necessary – even for a
neurosurgeon.

I was shocked to learn that the only ancient
languages he could read were Latin, Greek, and
Hebrew, and that he knows almost nothing of math-
ematics beyond the elementary levels of the calculus
of variations. When he admitted this to me, I found
myself almost annoyed. It was as if he'd hidden this
part of himself in order to deceive me, pretending – as
do many people I've discovered – to be what he is not.
No one I've ever known is what he appears to be on
the surface.

Dr Nemur appears to be uncomfortable around
me. Sometimes when I try to talk to him, he just
looks at me strangely and turns away. I was angry at
first when Dr Strauss told me I was giving Dr Nemur
an inferiority complex. I thought he was mocking me
and I'm oversensitive at being made fun of.

How was I to know that a highly respected psycho-
experimentalist like Nemur was unacquainted with
Hindustani and Chinese? It's absurd when you con-
sider the work that is being done in India and China
today in the very field of his study.

I asked Dr Strauss how Nemur could refute Ra-
hajamati's attack on his method and results if Nemur
couldn't even read them in the first place. That strange
look on Dr Strauss' face can mean only one of two
things. Either he doesn't want to tell Nemur what
they're saying in India, or else – and this worries me –
Dr Strauss doesn't know either. I must be careful to

speak and write clearly and simply so that people won't laugh.

May 18 I am very disturbed. I saw Miss Kinnian last night for the first time in over a week. I tried to avoid all discussions of intellectual concepts and to keep the conversation on a simple, everyday level, but she just stared at me blankly and asked me what I meant about the mathematical variance equivalent in Dorbermann's *Fifth Concerto*.

When I tried to explain she stopped me and laughed. I guess I got angry, but I suspect I'm approaching her on the wrong level. No matter what I try to discuss with her, I am unable to communicate. I must review Vrostadt's equations on *Levels of Semantic Progression*. I find that I don't communicate with people much any more. Thank God for books and music and things I can think about. I am alone in my apartment at Mrs Flynn's boardinghouse most of the time and seldom speak to anyone.

May 20 I would not have noticed the new dishwasher, a boy of about sixteen, at the corner diner where I take my evening meals if not for the incident of the broken dishes.

They crashed to the floor, shattering and sending bits of white china under the tables. The boy stood there, dazed and frightened, holding the empty tray in his hand. The whistles and catcalls from the customers (the cries of 'hey, there go the profits!' ...

'*Mazeltov!*' . . . and 'well, *he* didn't work here very long . . .' which invariably seems to follow the breaking of glass or dishware in a public restaurant) all seemed to confuse him.

When the owner came to see what the excitement was about, the boy cowered as if he expected to be struck and threw up his arms as if to ward off the blow.

'All right! All right, you dope,' shouted the owner, 'don't just stand there! Get the broom and sweep that mess up. A broom . . . a broom, you idiot! It's in the kitchen. Sweep up all the pieces.'

The boy saw that he was not going to be punished. His frightened expression disappeared and he smiled and hummed as he came back with the broom to sweep the floor. A few of the rowdier customers kept up the remarks, amusing themselves at his expense.

'Here, sonny, over here there's a nice piece behind you . . .'

'C'mon, do it again . . .'

'He's not so dumb. It's easier to break 'em than to wash 'em . . .'

As his vacant eyes moved across the crowd of amused onlookers, he slowly mirrored their smiles and finally broke into an uncertain grin at the joke which he obviously did not understand.

I felt sick inside as I looked at his dull, vacuous smile, the wide, bright eyes of a child, uncertain but eager to please. They were laughing at him because he was mentally retarded.

And I had been laughing at him too.

Suddenly, I was furious at myself and all those who were smirking at him. I jumped up and shouted, 'Shut up! Leave him alone! It's not his fault he can't understand! He can't help what he is! But for God's sake . . . he's still a human being!'

The room grew silent. I cursed myself for losing control and creating a scene. I tried not to look at the boy as I paid my bill and walked out without touching my food. I felt ashamed for both of us.

How strange it is that people of honest feelings and sensibility, who would not take advantage of a man born without arms or legs or eyes – how such people think nothing of abusing a man born with low intelligence. It infuriated me to think that not too long ago I, like this boy, had foolishly played the clown.

And I had almost forgotten.

I'd hidden the picture of the old Charlie Gordon from myself because now that I was intelligent it was something that had to be pushed out of my mind. But today in looking at that boy, for the first time I saw what I had been. *I was just like him!*

Only a short time ago, I learnt that people laughed at me. Now I can see that unknowingly I joined with them in laughing at myself. That hurts most of all.

I have often reread my progress reports and seen the illiteracy, the childish naiveté, the mind of low intelligence peering from a dark room, through the keyhole, at the dazzling light outside. I see that even in my dullness I knew that I was inferior, and that other people had something I lacked – something denied me. In my mental blindness, I thought that it was somehow connected with the ability to read and write, and I was sure that if I could get those skills I would automatically have intelligence too.

Even a feeble-minded man wants to be like other men.

A child may not know how to feed itself, or what to eat, yet it knows of hunger.

This then is what I was like, I never knew. Even with my gift of intellectual awareness, I never really knew.

This day was good for me. Seeing the past more clearly, I have decided to use my knowledge and skills to work in the field of increasing human intelligence levels. Who is better equipped for this work? Who else has lived in both worlds? These are my people. Let me use my gift to do something for them.

Tomorrow, I will discuss with Dr Strauss the manner in which I can work in this area. I may be able to help him work out the problems of widespread use of the technique which was used on me. I have several good ideas of my own.

There is so much that might be done with this technique. If I could be made into a genius, what about thousands of others like myself? What fantastic levels might be achieved by using this technique on normal people? On *geniuses*?

There are so many doors to open. I am impatient to begin.

Progress report 13

May 23 It happened today. Algernon bit me. I visited the lab to see him as I do occasionally, and when I took him out of his cage, he snapped at my hand. I put him back and watched him for a while. He was unusually disturbed and vicious.

May 24 Burt, who is in charge of the experimental animals, tells me that Algernon is changing. He is less co-operative; he refuses to run the maze any more; general motivation has decreased. And he hasn't been eating. Everyone is upset about what this may mean.

May 25 They've been feeding Algernon, who now refuses to work the shifting-lock problem. Everyone identifies me with Algernon. In a way we're both the first of our kind. They all pretending that Algernon's behaviour is not necessarily significant for me. But it's hard to hide the fact that some of the other animals who were used in this experiment are showing strange behaviour.

Dr Strauss and Dr Nemur have asked me not to come to the lab any more. I know what they're thinking but I can't accept it. I am going ahead with my plans to carry their research forward. With all due respect to both of these fine scientists, I am well aware of their limitations. If there is an answer, I'll have to find it out for myself. Suddenly, time has become very important to me.

★

May 29 I have been given a lab of my own and permission to go ahead with the research. I'm on to something. Working day and night. I've had a bed moved into the lab. Most of my writing time is spent on the notes which I keep in a separate folder, but from time to time I feel it necessary to put down my moods and my thoughts out of sheer habit.

I find the *calculus of intelligence*, to be a fascinating study. Here is the place for the application of all the knowledge I have acquired. In a sense it's the problem I've been concerned with all my life.

May 31 Dr Strauss thinks I'm working too hard. Dr Nemur says I'm trying to cram a lifetime of research and thought into a few weeks. I know I should rest, but I'm driven on by something inside that won't let me stop. I've got to find the reason for the sharp regression in Algernon. I've got to know *if* and *when* it will happen to me.

June 4

LETTER TO DR STRAUSS (*copy*)
Dear Dr Strauss:

Under separate cover I am sending you a copy of my report entitled, 'The Algernon–Gordon Effect: A Study of Structure and Function of Increased Intelligence,' which I would like to have you read and have published.

As you see, my experiments are completed. I have included in my report all of my formulae, as well as mathematical analysis in the appendix. Of course, these should be verified.

Because of its importance to both you and Dr Nemur (and need I say to myself, too?) I have checked and rechecked my results a dozen times in the hope of finding an error. I am sorry to say the results must stand. Yet for the sake of science, I am grateful for the little bit that I here add to the knowledge of the function of the human mind and of the laws governing the artificial increase of human intelligence.

I recall your once saying to me that an experimental *failure* or the *disproving* of a theory was as important to the advancement of learning as a success would be. I know now that this is true. I am, sorry, however, that my own contribution to the field must rest upon the ashes of the work of two men I regard so highly.

Yours truly,

Charles Gordon

encl: report.

June 5 I must not become emotional. The facts and the results of my experiments are clear, and the more sensational aspects of my own rapid climb cannot obscure the fact that the trippling of intelligence by the surgical technique developed by Drs Strauss and Nemur must be viewed as having little or no practical applicability (at the present time) to the increase of human intelligence.

As I review the records and data on Algernon, I see that although he is still in his physical infancy, he has regressed mentally. Motor activity is impaired; there is a general reduction of glandular activity; there is an accelerated loss of co–ordination.

There are also strong indications of progressive amnesia.

As will be seen by my report, these and other physical and mental deterioration syndromes can be predicted with statistically significant results by the application of my formula.

The surgical stimulus to which we were both sub-jected has resulted in an intensification and acceleration of all mental processes. The unforeseen development, which I have taken the liberty of calling the *Algernon-Gordon Effect*, is the logical extension of the entire intelligence speed–up. The hypothesis here proven may be described simply in the following terms: Artificially increased intelligence deteriorates at a rate of time directly proportional to the quantity of the increase.

I feel that this, in itself, is an important discovery.

As long as I am able to write, I will continue to record my thoughts in these progress reports. It is one of my few pleasures. However, by all indications, my own mental deterioration will be very rapid.

I have already begun to notice signs of emotional instability and forgetfulness, the first symptoms of the burnout.

June 10 Deterioration progressing. I have become

absentminded. Algernon died two days ago. Dissection shows my predictions were right. His brain had decreased in weight and there was a general smoothing out of cerebral convolutions as well as a deepening and broadening of brain fissures.

I guess the same thing is or will soon be happening to me. Now that it's definite, I don't want it to happen.

I put Algernon's body in a cheese box and buried him in the backyard. I cried.

June 15 Dr Strauss came to see me again. I wouldn't open the door and I told him to go away. I want to be left to myself. I have become touchy and irritable. I feel the darkness closing in. It's hard to throw off thoughts of suicide. I keep telling myself how important this introspective journal will be.

It's a strange sensation to pick up a book that you've read and enjoyed just a few months ago and discover that you don't remember it. I remembered how great I thought John Milton was, but when I picked up *Paradise Lost* I couldn't understand it at all. I got so angry I threw the book across the room.

I'v got to try to hold on to some of it. Some of the things I've learnt. Oh God, please don't take it all away.

June 19 Sometimes, at night, I go out for a walk. Last night I couldn't remember where I lived. A policeman took me home. I have the strange feeling that this has all happened to me before – a long time ago. I keep telling myself I'm the only person in the world who can describe what's happening to me.

June 21 Why can't I remember? I've got to fight. I lie in bed for days and I don't know who or where I am. Then it all comes back to me in a flash. Fugues of amnesia. Symptoms of senility – second childhood. I can watch them coming on. It's so cruelly logical. I learnt so much and so fast. Now my mind is deteriorating rapidly. I won't let it happen. I'll fight it. I can't help thinking of the boy in the restaurant, the blank expression, the silly smile, the people laughing at him. No – please – not that again . . .

June 22 I'm forgetting things that I learnt recently. It seems to be following the classic pattern – the last things learnt are the first things forgotten. Or is that the pattern? I'd better look it up again . . .

I reread my paper on the *Algernon-Gordon Effect* and I get the strange feeling that it was written by someone else. There are parts I don't even understand.

Motor activity impaired. I keep tripping over things, and it becomes increasingly difficult to type.

June 23 I've given up using the typewriter completely. My co-ordination is bad. I feel that I'm moving slower and slower. Had a terrible shock today. I picked up a copy of an article I used in my research, Krueger's *Uber psychische Ganzheit*, to see if it would help me understand what I had done. First I thought there was something wrong with my eyes. Then I realized I could no longer read German. I tested myself in other languages. All gone.

June 30 A week since I dared to write again. It's slipping away like sand through my fingers. Most of the books I have are too hard for me now. I get angry with them because I know that I read and understood them just a few weeks ago.

I keep telling myself I must keep writing these reports so that somebody will know what is happening to me. But it gets harder to form the words and remember spellings. I have to look up even simple words in the dictionary now and it makes me impatient with myself.

Dr Strauss comes around almost every day, but I told him I wouldn't see or speak to anybody. He feels guilty. They all do. But I don't blame anyone. I knew what might happen. But how it hurts.

July 7 I don't know where the week went. Todays Sunday I know because I can see through my window people going to church. I think I stayed in bed all week but I remember Mrs Flynn bringing food to me a few times. I keep saying over and over I've got to do something but then I forget or maybe its just easier not to do what I say Im going to do.

I think of my mother and father a lot these days. I found a picture of them with me taken at a beach. My father has a big ball under his arm and my mother is holding me by the hand. I dont remember them the way they are in the picture. All I remember is my father drunk most of the time and arguing with mum about money.

He never shaved much and he used to scratch my face when he hugged me. My mother said he died but Cousin Miltie said he heard his mum and dad say that my father ran away with another woman. When I asked my mother she slapped my face and said my father was dead. I dont think I ever found out which was true but I don't care much. (He said he was going to take me to see cows on a farm once but he never did. He never kept his promises . . .)

July 10 My landlady Mrs Flynn is very worried about me. She says the way I lay around all day and dont do anything I remind her of her son before she threw him out of the house. She said she doesnt like loafers. If Im sick its one thing, but if Im a loafer thats another thing and she wont have it. I told her I think Im sick.

I try to read a little bit every day, mostly stories, but sometimes I have to read the same thing over and over again because I don't know what it means. And its hard to write. I know I should look up all the words in the dictionary but its so hard and Im so tired all the time.

Then I got the idea that I would only use the easy words instead of the long hard ones. That saves time.

I put flowers on Algernons grave about once a week. Mrs Flynn thinks Im crazy to put flowers on a mouses grave but I told her that Algernon was special.

July 14 Its sunday again. I dont have anything to do to keep me busy now because my television set is broke and I dont have any money to get it fixed. (I think I lost this months check from the lab. I dont remember)

I get awful headaches and asperin doesnt help me much. Mrs Flynn knows Im really sick and she feels very sorry for me. Shes a wonderful woman whenever someone is sick.

July 22 Mrs Flynn called a strange doctor to see me. She was afraid I was going to die. I told the doctor I wasnt too sick and that I only forget sometimes. He asked me did I have any friends or relatives and I said no I dont have any. I told him I had a friend called Algernon once but he was a mouse and we used to run races together. He looked at me kind of funny like he thought I was crazy.

He smiled when I told him I used to be a genius. He talked to me like I was a baby and he winked at Mrs Flynn. I got mad and chased him out because he was making fun of me the way they all used to.

July 24 I have no more money and Mrs Flynn says I got to go to work somewhere and pay the rent because I havent paid for over two months. I dont know any work but the job I used to have at Donnegans Plastic Box Company. I dont want to go back there because they all knew me when I was smart and maybe theyll laugh at me. But I dont know what else to do to get money.

July 25 I was looking at some of my old progress reports and its very funny but I cant read what I wrote. I can make out some of the words but they dont make sense.

Miss Kinnian came to the door but I said go away I dont want to see you. She cried and I cried too but I wouldnt let her in because I didnt want her to laugh at me. I told her I didn't like her any more. I told her I didnt want to be smart any more. Thats not true. I still love her and I still want to be smart but I had to say that so shed go away. She gave Mrs Flynn money to pay the rent. I dont want that. I got to get a job.

Please . . . please let me not forget how to read and write . . .

July 27 Mr Donnegan was very nice when I came back and asked him for my old job of janitor. First he was very suspicious but I told him what happened to me then he looked very sad and put his hand on my shoulder and said Charlie Gordon you got guts.

Everybody looked at me when I came downstairs and started working in the toilet sweeping it out like I used to. I told myself Charlie if they make fun of you dont get sore because you remember their not so smart as you once thot they were. And besides they were once your friends and if they laughed at you that doesnt mean anything because they liked you too.

One of the new men who came to work there after I went away made a nasty crack. he said hey Charlie I heat your a very smart fella a real quiz kid. Say something intelligent. I felt bad but Joe Carp came over and grabbed him by the shirt and said leave him alone you lousy cracker or Ill break your neck. I didn't expect Joe to take my part so I guess hes really my friend.

Later Frank Reilly came over and said Charlie if anybody bothers you or trys to take advantage you call me or Joe and we will set em straight. I said thanks Frank and I got choked up so I had to turn around and go into the supply room so he wouldnt see me cry. Its good to have friends.

July 28 I did a dumb thing today I forgot I wasnt in Miss Kinnians class at the adult center any more like I use to be. I went in and sat down in my old seat in the back of the room and she looked at me funny and she said Charles. I didnt remember she ever called me that before only Charlie so I said hello Miss Kinnian Im ready for my lesin today only I lost my reader that we was using. She startid to cry and run out of the room and everybody looked at me and I saw they wasnt the same pepul who used to be in my class.

Then all of a suddin I rememberd some things about the operashun and me getting smart and I said holy smoke I reely pulled a Charlie Gordon that time. I went away before she come back to the room.

Thats why Im going away from New York for good. I dont want to do nothing like that agen. I dont want Miss Kinnian to feel sorry for me. Evry body feels sorry at the factery and I dont want that eather so Im going someplace where nobody knows that Charlie Gordon was once a genus and now he cant even reed a book or rite good.

Im taking a cuple of books along and even if I cant reed them Ill practise hard and maybe I wont forget everything I lerned. If I try reel hard maybe Ill be a little bit smarter then I was before the operashun. I got my rabits foot and my luky penny and maybe they will help me.

If you ever reed this Miss Kinnian dont be sorry for me Im glad I got a second chanse to be smart because I learned a lot of things that I never even new were in this world and Im grateful that I saw it all for a little bit. I dont know why Im dumb agen or what I did wrong maybe its because I didnt try hard enuff. But if I try and practis very hard maybe Ill get a littl smarter and know what all the words are. I remember a little bit how nice I had a feeling with the blue book that has the torn cover when I red it. Thats why Im gonna keep trying to get smart so I can have that feeling agen. Its a good feeling to know things and be smart. I wish I had it rite now if I did I would sit down and reed all the time. Anyway I bet Im the first dumb person in the world who ever found out something important for sience. I remember I did somthing but I dont remember what. So I gess its like I did it for all the dumb pepul like me.

Good-by Miss Kinnian and Dr Strauss and evreybody. And P.S. please tell Dr Nemur not to be such a grouch when pepul laff at him and he woud have more frends. Its easy to make frends if you let pepul laff at you. Im going to have lots of frends where I go.

P.P.S. Please if you get a chanse put some flowrs on Algernons grave in the bak yard . . .

Acknowledgements

The editor and publishers gratefully acknowledge the following for permission to reproduce copyright material in this book:

'Confluence' by Brian Aldiss from *The Moment of Eclipse*, published by Faber & Faber Ltd, 1970, copyright © Brian W. Aldiss, 1967, reprinted by permission of the author; 'Will we be judged' from The New Testament: Revelations, extracts from the Authorized Version of the Bible (the King James Bible), the rights in which are vested in the Crown, reproduced by permission of the Crown's Patentee, Cambridge University Press; 'There Will Come Soft Rains' by Ray Bradbury, copyright © Ray Bradbury, reprinted by permission of Abner Stein; 'Of Polymuf Stock' by John Christopher from *Young Winter's Tales no. 2*, published by Macmillan, copyright © John Christopher, 1971, reprinted by permission of the author; 'The Nine Billion Names of God' by Arthur C. Clark from *Of Time and Stars*, first published by Victor Gollancz Ltd, copyright © Arthur C. Clark, 1972, reprinted by permission of the author and the author's agents, Scott Meredith Literary Agency Inc., 845 Third Avenue, New York, New York 10022 and David Higham Associates; 'Flowers for Algernon' copyright © 1959, 1987 by Daniel Keyes, reprinted by permission of the author; 'Captain Courage and the Rose Street Gang' by Jan Mark from *Out of Time* edited by Aidan Chambers, published by The Bodley Head Ltd, copyright © Jan Mark, 1983, reprinted by permission of Murray Pollinger; 'The Space Merchants' by Pohl/Kornbluth, published by Ballantine Books, copyright © Rediffusion Television Ltd, 1952, 1953, reprinted by permission of Pamela Buckmaster of Carnell Literary Agency on behalf of the authors; 'Harrison Bergeron' by Kurt Vonnegut, first published in *Magazine of Fantasy and Science Fiction*, copyright © Kurt Vonnegut Jr, 1961, reprinted by permission of Donald C. Farber, Attorney for Mr Vonnegut; 'The Destruction of Weybridge and Shepperton' by H. G. Wells from *The War of the Worlds*, published by Heinemann, copyright © The Literary Executors of the Estate of H. G. Wells, 1898, reprinted by permission of A. P. Watt Ltd.